Into the Enchanted Forest

ALICIA J. CHUMNEY

Copyright © 2016 by Alicia J. Chumney All rights reserved.

This book or any portion thereof may not be reproduced or used in any manner whatsoever without the express written permission of the publisher except for the use of brief quotations in a book review.

Cover Design: Jennifer Ayres
Editor: Rachel D. Moore

1. Young Adult 2. New Adult 3. Fantasy/Fairy Tale
   First Edition

Dedication

Once again for my friends for the many times I asked for name suggestions and their support.

For Rachel D. Moore for her thorough Beta Read.

Table of Contents

_Toc38286584
Part One	6
Prologue	7
Chapter 1	19
Chapter 2	38
Chapter 3	48
Chapter 4	58
Chapter 5	69
Chapter 6	77
Chapter 7	88
Chapter 8	100
Chapter 9	107
Chapter 10	112
Chapter 11	117
Chapter 12	122
Chapter 13	127
Part Two	131
Chapter 14	132
Chapter 15	143
Chapter 16	148
Chapter 17	165
Chapter 18	168
Chapter 19	171
Chapter 20	180
Chapter 21	187
Chapter 22	192
Chapter 23	200

Chapter 24	209
Chapter 25	217
Chapter 26	236
Chapter 27	241
ALSO AVAILABLE BY THIS AUTHOR:	247
ABOUT THE AUTHOR	249

Part One

Prologue

Holding the squirming two-year-old in her arms, the Queen tried to keep her tears to a minimum. Her husband had already left the room with their son and the Spade suspected that the King was using the boy as an excuse to leave the room and to keep his wife from seeing his own tears. Sending their youngest child off to be fostered in another world was terrifying.

His own youngest son, Ethan Jackson, was standing at attention in only the way that a six-year-old could manage – mostly tall and still but with the occasional twitch and fidget, his dark hair managing to fall over his forehead no matter how often the boy tried to fix it. His other sons were somewhere else dealing with their own tasks, but the Spade knew that Ethan would meet the Princess again one day. They needed the boy around to be able to identify the Princess later thanks to the magical bond that would form once the Queen handed the toddler over to his son.

Before they had even left their cottage, the Spade had explained to his son the way things would be done. He told him about the magical bond that would form between the children in order to make things easier for Ethan to be able to track the Princess when it was time to bring her home.

He did not tell his son that there was a slim possibility that there could be more to their magical bond than just being able to track the Princess in nineteen years. Looking over at his tearful Queen, he was more than thankful that True Love was enough to mostly break their bond, even though the Queen frequently asked her trusty Spade for advice.

But he also knew that Ethan would not become a Card and that could change everything.

Nineteen Years Later

He had forgotten about his tracking bond to the Princess until his father had called him for duty. Normally, Henry the Heart would summon him for family things, so getting a message from his father was intriguing enough on its own. When the retired Spade sent his youngest son a message that Jack needed to meet with him about a task it meant that Ethan needed to drop everything and appear before the Spade.

Ethan Samuel Jackson was a man of many names and he was informally known as Jack Huntsman by his associates and colleagues. The last thing the Huntsman was expecting was to find himself standing in formation in front of his father the Retired Spade, his brother the Heart, and the Queen Alice the Fifth of Wonderland.

Standing tall, the Queen addressed him, "Almost nineteen years ago you and your father traveled with my daughter into another world on a mission. It is time for you to track down the Harrington's and bring back my daughter. Her twenty-first birthday is quickly approaching and she will need a familiar face if she is to take on the trials of the Enchanted Forest."

The Queen's speech triggered a faint memory from when he was six-years-old and holding the hand of a tiny girl as they led her to and through the Portals of the Worlds and handed her over to her adoptive parents in a land called "Earth" or "The Real World".

"Your Majesty, was I wrong in thinking that the Princess will turn twenty-one in a few months?" Jack asked, wondering why he could not leave closer to the big day.

"Yes, she does, but I doubt that she will trust a virtual stranger who approaches her on the first full day of her twenty-first year and tells her that she is a Princess of Wonderland and must return home as quickly as possible."

The Spade looked at the Queen before nodding his head. "It is a well-keep secret that the Queen is dying and it is imperative that the next Wonderland heir is found and quickly taught what she needs to learn about the kingdom."

This tracking business was a tad more difficult than his father had warned him about.

First, there was the daunting task of creating a portal in a location that would not be obvious but was close enough to the Princess' last known address. Ethan had no special Card magic, but his father insisted that he try, knowing that his son was still the Princess' Tracker and that was magic enough.

After waving his arm and reciting the words that had been carefully written down on the strip of paper in front of him, the Huntsman stared amazed at the translucent portal in front of him.

"How?" he asked, the final syllables trailing off in amazement.

"You are Princess Gabrielle's Tracker and with that responsibility comes Tracker magic. You will keep it until the Princess crosses back over the Wonderland Bridge," his father explained.

The explanation still felt lacking as his father forced him through the portal, reminding him to not lose that tiny piece of paper. "You'll need it to create the portal you will both return through," was the last thing he heard his father say before he found himself in the middle of a wooded area.

Finding the Harrington's would not be the problem; they had not moved from the very house where they had raised Gabrielle since her second birthday. It was finding the Princess that was the problem.

"She's in college," Michaela Harrington stammered, surprised to see the six-foot-three "Ethan Clark" in her doorway asking about her 'adoptive' daughter. "We couldn't stop her from going. It's her Junior Year!"

Nodding his head, Jack started to wonder how he was going to get into college.

Turning around quickly, a question occurred to him. "Does the Princess know she's adopted?"

Holding his wife close to him as she sobbed, knowing what the appearance of this Tracker meant, Preston simply nodded his head. "We let her know as soon as she was old enough to understand what we were telling her."

Somehow, even now he was not entirely certain that it had been magic or luck, he found himself sitting next to the girl in some college English Literature class. It only took a little bit of magic to help prevent the professor from calling on him to answer any questions. That tiny enchantment was a good thing because Jack found it difficult to focus on anything other than the Princess sitting right next to him.

"Oral traditions are a major part of storytelling. The average person was incapable of reading; it was a luxury that many couldn't afford since they spent their days working and tending towards their families. But at night and during festivals and other special occasions the storytellers would come out and tell the tales that they had learned. What types of literary devices were used in order to help the troubadours learn the epics they often told or sung?"

No, Jack was careful to ensure that nobody would really notice that he was not answering any questions or taking notes on stories that he did not really care about. Certainly, he did the occasional reading, but his motives were anything but the pursuit of knowledge.

It did not change the irritating fact that he felt the unexplainable desire to gain the Princess's approval.

The pounding beat was giving her a headache. She couldn't believe that she had let her closest friends drag her to a night club on her birthday. Well, technically her birthday was still in an hour. Her parents had been very careful to remind her that she didn't technically turn twenty-one until 11:27 pm. Then her mother had burst into tears and sobbed something about the past nineteen years having gone by too fast. Her father had added to the weirdness by telling her how proud he was of how she'd grown into a mature and polite young lady.

"Hey," one of her friends slurred, "isn't that the hot guy that's in several of your classes?" Gabby followed the unsteady finger that pointed in Ethan Clark's direction.

"Yeah," she mumbled a response before taking a sip of her drink.

"You should go ask him to dance."

Shaking her head, Gabby turned away from his unnerving gaze before looking at her friends. All she wanted to do was count down the hours until she could make her excuses and leave. Everybody knew that she would rather be curled up with a book and a cup of tea than out dancing and drinking.

What she did not know was that Ethan Clark had been carefully steering the more troublesome of the males flirting with their group carefully in other directions. He was painstakingly counting down the hours until he could return home.

It started off as any other normal Thursday. One moment Gabrielle "Gabby" Harrington was walking down the sidewalk heading towards her 9:30 English Literature class.

The sidewalk was tree-lined and with her earbuds in place to help block the outside world she barely noticed that the trees were getting closer and closer together. Even the sidewalk was changing from concrete to pebble gravel and then into a dirt path.

Looking up from her book she finally realized two things: she was no longer on campus and her general feeling of being out of place was gone. Looking around her, even spinning around in a circle in hopes that what she was seeing wasn't truly happening; she could only take stock of the unfamiliar surroundings. Anything else at that moment might result in screaming or worse, tears.

It was difficult to determine which scenario was more disturbing.

Gabby could have sworn that all she had done was walk towards her class. She wasn't even hungover from her 21st birthday celebration the night before. There were no white rabbits with watches catching her attention. There were no holes in the ground where she could have stumbled into them. There were no mirrors hanging on any walls or trees. She was not still asleep in her bed like many of the students on campus.

Instead, she was standing in the middle of what could only be a deserted town square and she was wearing a red cloak of all things.

She didn't know where to start.

"Don't most dreams begin by falling asleep?" Gabby whispered to herself, reluctant to disturb the unsettled silence around her. "At least I didn't have to fall down a rabbit hole."

"The original Alice did," a familiar voice from behind her stated, making her jump, "but you are wearing a red cloak too."

Spinning around, she stopped just in time to see Ethan Clark emerging from the trees. "Aren't you in my English class?" The last person she expected to see was the very good-looking guy who was in at least three of her five classes.

"Yes, technically am I."

Scanning him from head to foot, taking in the messy dark hair and well-worn jeans, she hoped his appearance belied his abilities. "Toto, I've a feeling we're not in Kansas anymore," Gabby quoted.

"Who is Toto? We were not in Kansas to begin with…"

Gabby started to laugh at the bewildered expression on Ethan's face and the stilted way he occasionally talked.

"It's a movie quote. It means I'm no longer home."

"Of course, you are home. At least you are nearly home. Welcome to The Enchanted Forest, Your Majesty," he greeted her, executing a perfect bow before her.

"Wonderland should be that way," he smiled as he pointed vaguely down the road in front of them. "I think."

Chapter 1

It was information overload and Gabby thought that finals week was rough. There were so many questions jumbled around in her head and she didn't really want to acknowledge the one question that was the most important.

Why did she need a bodyguard?

Did he really say The Enchanted Forest?

Why was he her bodyguard?

Did she really just spot a pink castle through the trees?

Did he just call her 'Your Majesty' and take a bow?

"Why am I wearing a red cloak?"

Jack blinked in shock. That was not the question he was expecting. "You are the daughter of Queen Alice the Fifth of Wonderland. Her great-great-great-grandmother times several more was Queen Alice the First. She married one of the other Kings of Wonderland and eventually they had a son and daughter. That daughter had a daughter named Queen Alice the Second. This Alice married Red

Riding Hood's son. They had a son and a daughter. The daughter became Queen and the son a Huntsman."

Jack took a deep breath before continuing. He hated having to go through the dull and dry information to explain to the Princess about her family tree. "The Alice line runs through the daughters."

Stumbling slightly, Gabby said the only thing that she fully grasped from his recitation, "So I'm a princess."

"Yes," he dryly answered her, cutting down on the charm he had used to gain her trust during the semester.

Nodding her head, Gabby moved to the next thought in her head. She found it easier to work through things in a linear fashion instead of attempting to follow the tangled mess of thoughts all vying for her attention. "That's why I need a bodyguard."

"Yes."

Gabby just blinked. It was a lot of information to take in at one time. It was a lot of information to sort through. It was a lot of information that she should have been told long before she turned twenty-one.

Like the fact that she was a princess. Of a place she had previously thought to be fictional.

Finally, she asked the question that was pestering her to be answered more than any other question, "What about my parents?"

Jack refused to show his confusion. "The King and Queen?"

Gabby moved to sit on a log, forcing Jack to stop walking. Once he rejoined her, she clarified her question, "No, the people that raised me. My adoptive parents. Did they know?"

Jack did not want to have to answer this particular question. Protecting her he could do. He was currently doing exactly that as he scanned the surrounding area for potential threats while she learned more about herself than she ever thought possible.

"They 'adopted' you when you were two years old. Foster might be a better term. They knew that they would have you until your twenty-first birthday. As soon as you walked through that portal the only evidence that you ever existed in that world is at the Harrington house. Only they will remember you."

She started to cry and all Jack could do was sit down and pull her into a hug. He felt awkward standing in position while his charge bawled her heart out. He felt awkward wrapping her in a hug. It went against all of his training as a Huntsman and as a Spare Card.

Minutes that felt like hours later, she calmed down and asked her next question. "Why are you my bodyguard? You look like you aren't that much older than me. You said that you were an Army brat at school."

"I am 25 years old and I was tasked with protecting you at college until it was time to bring you home. My father, the Retired Spade, knew I might have to look like I was college-age in order to blend into my surroundings and my older brothers were too old for the task. I will be your bodyguard until we return to the castle and an older guard can be put in place, probably my eldest brother, Henry or Stephan. This was a task given to me when I was six years old and what I've been training for along with my Huntsman duties."

She wanted to hit him because of the clinical way that he talked, all proper and dry. "Why not you? If you've been trained to be one of my bodyguards since you were six years old, why wouldn't you continue with the job once I was returned to my rightful place?" The end of her sentence left a slightly bitter taste in her mouth.

"I am the fifth Jack and you can only have four Jacks. My primary job is a Huntsman although I have had Card Training as a Jack."

Gabby started to get up and walk. She couldn't stay in one place a moment longer. All of Jack's answers gave her even more questions and she would rather be moving instead of letting everything make her even more confused and tangled.

A few things had started making sense like her fascination with the *Alice* novels that her mother put in front of her when she was eight.

When she was twelve, she swore she saw a green cat in the mirror, but it quickly faded away before she could turn around and get a second look. There had also been a green hooded sweatshirt hanging up behind her and Gabby chalked the whole vision up to reading too late at night when she should have been asleep.

She thought she had imaged the chess pieces in her father's study moving on their own accord, but not in any fashion that she recognized from when she had been taught to play. The chess pieces had been moving backward! It had given her the idea to see if they could play chess backward.

When she was a teenager, she devoured any *Alice in Wonderland* variation that she could get her hands on, even the dirty ones.

That same year she had wanted a white rabbit as a pet even though her father refused her simple request.

Even with her knowledge of the *Alice* books, she was well aware that there were no Huntsmen in the cannon. *Little Red Riding Hood* maybe, but not in *Alice in Wonderland*.

"Huntsman?"

Jack had hoped that the questions would end soon, but he could not complain because they had started walking again. He knew there would be a chance that Gabby would ask a lot of questions; research indicated that she came about her nickname honestly. "They guard Wonderland and The Enchanted Forest. They are like an army. Their ranks are mostly hereditary, most of them being your cousins, but there are volunteers."

"So, if you are a Huntsman that makes us cousins?"

"No, I am a volunteer," Jack laughed. "Your cousins make certain that everything runs smoothly. They handle assignments, who goes where, does what, that sort of thing. They handle the paperwork bureaucracy and stay in positions where they can remain safe. The Huntsmen themselves go out into the field and keep things like werewolves under control. We are not related. My family line is part of the royal guard – the Jackson's or "Jacks" – are bodyguards. I am the fifth Jackson but traditionally there are only supposed to be four Jacks. I think my mother was hoping for a Jill. Regardless, my older brothers – you will meet them as Heart, Club, Spade, and Diamond – are the Queen's Jacks and I decided to become a Huntsman. My original last name became my first and my new last name became Hunt. My full name is Ethan Samuel Jackson Hunt and until I decided to become a Huntsman, I was called Extra."

"Why Extra? Wait, isn't your last name is Clark." Gabby asked, intentionally paying more attention to Jack than the road and trees around them; they all looked the same to her anyway. At least this way things could seem more as if they were taking a hike through the woods on a date – not that she'd let him know she's once fantasied about him asking her out – instead of heading in the vague direction of Wonderland.

"I lied about my real name in your adopted world just in case anybody recognized me or did not forget about my existence there. I am called Extra because I am the extra Jack. My brothers took on the role that matched their first initial too; Henry, Charlie, Stephan, and Derek. Step is really nervous because my middle initial is an S, but he's forgetting that my mother had a design; Derek also has the middle initial S." Jack rambled, trying to keep Gabrielle distracted from the way that the trees were starting to press on in each other and that the road was becoming rockier. She didn't seem to notice the changes to the landscape. It could be a problem later.

For the first time, Gabby realized that she found somebody who could talk just as much as she could. "You talk a lot," she blurted out.

Shaking his head, Jack carefully worded his response, "Yes, I do. I have a lot to explain to you. Is that a problem?"

"No, it's fine," Gabby conceded. "It means I don't have to think about all of this yet."

"But you will have to," Jack stated, "You are wearing a red hooded cloak and that is normally a sign of what is going to come your way. Then there is the fact that this place is not going to let you ascend the throne without going through your own tale."

"What? Defeat an evil wolf and live happily ever after with the Huntsman who saves me?" Gabby flippantly asked, not completely serious and mentally flinching at what she had just said if he did take her jest seriously.

Not that it would be such a bad thing.

Maybe she wasn't over that short-lived fantasy after all.

Hiding his reaction as a good Card would do, "No, I am a Jackson; Jacks do not marry Alice's or Red's." He lied to himself when he ignored the fact that the statement appealed to his inner self.

Not knowing when to shut up, Gabby let her mouth run away with her, "But you are a Huntsman and you just told me that a Huntsman did marry a Red whose son married an Alice."

"I am the extra Jack. If something happens to one of my brothers then I become the Spade until Henry the Heart marries and has four sons. Unless Charlie becomes the Heart or Henry never marries then Charlie's boys become the Jacks, otherwise they are tens."

Her head began to spin with information overload; information that was not even about her own family. "Stephan's are all nines?" It was the only part of his explanation that she was able to grasp onto. She wanted to dismiss it all as being 'math', but the reality was that there was just too much new information for Gabby to process all in the hour that they had been walking.

"Derek's are eights and my children would be sevens if I ever marry. We have a younger sister named Jill; her sons are sixes. That is unless we have to rearrange our order due to some unforeseen incident."

Glancing quickly at the trees surrounding them, he noticed that they were giant oaks. It appeared that they were miles away from the pine trees at the center of the forest where they had landed even though it felt like only thirty minutes had passed since they entered the Enchanted Forest. He suspected that they had been walking for longer than either of them suspected. Time was a trickster in the Enchanted Forest.

"Jack and Jill went up a hill to fetch a pail of water," Gabby recited dryly after a few minutes of silence between the two of them as she took the time to process what Jack had been telling her. Instead, all she could come up with was a silly nursery rhyme.

The quip told her that too many serious thoughts were pressing down and fighting for attention and she still didn't want to acknowledge any of them. She still hadn't mentally addressed the fact that he had addressed her as "Your Majesty." At least she hadn't addressed it verbally.

"Please, do not remind me. My head still hurts when I remember that accident." Jack rubbed the back of his head at the memory as if the spot on his head still ached. It was difficult to tell if he was joking or serious. She went with serious because his demeanor had yet to crack since they had landed in this never-ending forest.

Gabby looked over at him while trying to decide which thought she wanted to entertain next. Finding out that nursery rhymes might also be real was starting to make her freak out just a little bit. "Who makes up five through two? Or the Aces?" That seemed like the least loaded question that she could ask.

"Sweetheart," Jack slipped, "your family is the Aces. Normally six through two are volunteer ranks if the current Jackson family does not have enough offspring. Four each is the rule."

"Four?"

"Like the card deck."

"My father, my mother, me, and…?"

"…Your brother."

"I have a brother? Is he a Huntsman?"

Jack laughed, "No, Gareth is married to a Wendy."

"As in *Peter Pan*? How can *Alice in Wonderland*, Little Red Riding Hood, and *Peter Pan* all be connected?"

"They are all children's stories. A story has to become a timeless classic children's story to get a thread in this world."

"So, Oz exists too?" Gabby's head was beginning to hurt and her bags – including her purse with her pain pills - had all disappeared when she arrived in The Enchanted Forest

"Yes, but Oz is harder to get to since they were cloaked in the original story; nobody knows how to get there. They can only leave. Fairy Tale Land, where we are, is the questing lands. It is more commonly known as The Enchanted Forest. Each major tale with a royal family has a castle located in a certain area and the others like Red Riding Hood and Hansel and Gretel can take place anywhere within the Forest boundaries. Oz, Wonderland, Neverland, etc, specific Quests only happen within those boundaries."

"So, there is a magic door?" She imagined something like in her one of her favorite television shows. Suddenly her likes were beginning to make sense.

He thought hard for a moment until he could come up with the best description, "Think more along the line of floating islands with bridges." Even that wasn't completely accurate. The 'islands' did not technically float. Some of the stories required staircases to get to their lands. One of the stories required a raft or a boat, but more used bridges and it was easier to explain things simply.

Reality once again returned and Gabby had stopped looking at Jack as they talked. "And people can travel freely between these lands?"

"For the most part; there are some places that you do not want to go." That did not stop Jack from looking at her. He was looking at everything, including his princess, for a slight hint of distress or an up-coming quest.

"Why?"

"There can be anything on these islands from Talking Animals, unexplored additions, or new additions mostly. That's really why Alice's, Wendy's, and a few other tales send their future rulers to Earth so that they can help identify these new lands when they return."

"So, I could go to Green Gables?" She thought back on one of her other favorite stories as a girl.

"I would not advise it; stories set in real worlds like *Anne of Green Gables* are on more of a time loop. If you get pulled into the story you have to wait it out until the end of the story or in this example series. You cannot permanently change the story, but one of Cinderella's princesses was curious and she has been gone for almost twenty years now. The current Cinderella, Eleanor, thankfully already had a second daughter and she is being trained as a future ruler just in case her first daughter does not make it back in time."

"So, no Harry Potter either?" Gabby said sadly.

Looking at the Princess carefully, he asked her something that had puzzled him and the other Huntsmen for years. "Is that the one with the magic school and the Quidditch?"

Jerking her head in his direction, Gabby wondered how he had learned about Hogwarts and Quidditch. "Yes, how did you know?"

Releasing a sigh at finding out that she would be able to identify at least one of the new story lands, Jack carefully explained, "A Number Two Diamond just returned from there. He was thankfully only gone six months but he told us about the battle of the school. We have been waiting and hoping you can tell us the entire story."

"Why is it on a time loop?" She had her suspicions but wanted him to confirm them.

Again, he started to put back some of the distance between then that had started to shorten once he realized that she was a well-read princess. "It takes place in England and the Elders decided to magically set it on a time loop until we knew what the story was about."

"Keep it on the loop for the time being," Gabby suggested after some thought. "It'll be a seven-year loop, but I'm not entirely certain yet if the story would be completely safe to enter into randomly."

She paused walking and looked around for the first time since they had left the town in the center of the forest. "How much longer until we reach Wonderland?" The trees were extremely close together and things were beginning to look creepy with all of the shadows lurking around every corner and behind every tree trunk.

"We are in the Enchanted Forest; the Forest is deciding your tale before directing us further. All we can do is walk and wait until the Forest decides on your trials. You might be an Alice Princess but you have a Goldilocks, a Gretel, and even a Little Mermaid prince – your father in fact - in your bloodlines."

She was curious about his answer to her next question. It would reveal so much about her new home. "Disney or Grimm Brothers Little Mermaid?"

Somehow managing to keep regret from his expression, Jack answered her, "Grimm Brothers I am afraid. Disney versions do not stick around here because they have not been around as long as the Grimm Tales." He had watched most of the Disney movies while he was shadowing Gabby and regretted that the original tales had taken such deep roots into the Forest's being. There was no telling when something would happen that could be as dark and gory as the Grimm tales.

"That was not a wise pairing," she whispered.

Jack was too relieved to discover that she knew some of the original fairy tales but resisted the urge to drill her knowledge. "I know, but it was True Love and messing with that is even worse than something bad happening to an offspring…"

Interrupting him, "Wait, my mother is the woman that Little Mermaid's Prince fell in love with…" She hated knowing what the implications were if her mother was matched with another tale's ruler.

"Thankfully it was his younger brother. Prince Eriksons cannot leave their boundaries and the firstborn son has to relive the story each generation."

"And me?"

"Prince Eriksons cannot marry a Princess in line for her own throne; it is that way in most of the lands. Only Prince Eriksons, Cinderella's Prince, and Snow White's Prince own their own thrones. There is another prince that maintains a kingdom, but I cannot recall who it is right now. Snow White has evolved to be the younger sister of another Princess and we do not get many step-mothers amongst the Royal Families anymore; just in the minor tales so sometimes a Snow White or Cinderella will pop up amongst them."

"Wasn't Cinderella's Prince the one with the throne in that tale? But earlier you said that a Cinderella was being trained for the crown?" Gabby was beginning to realize that not everything in the Enchanted Forest was obvious.

"That is complicated. There are Cinderella quests, but they are mostly to help Cinderella sons and daughters find their potential significant other. Only on occasion does a Cinderella tale occur, but it is always obvious."

Letting out a deep sigh as this new batch of information started setting in, Gabby stated, "This is complicated."

Looking at Gabby and not at the path in front of them, Jack broke and grinned at the princess. "Just do not cross any bridge that has a red rope over it and you will be fine."

At that moment the road ended at a bridge with a red rope. Looking back behind them, the road had vanished, leaving them surrounded by the trees that were close enough that nobody and nothing could fit between them. They could only move forward.

Cautiously, Gabby hoped he already knew the answer to her question. "What bridge is this?"

His face dropping back into the Jack mask, his regretful tone was the only indicator that he felt something. "Unexplored I am afraid," he sighed.

"Do I have to go alone?" She closed her eyes and hoped the opposite.

Standing tall and steady – he had stopped fidgeting when he was ten – the brave Jack plastered on his bodyguard persona before answering her. "I was sent to you because I am both a Jack and a Huntsman. Until you are safely in your castle, I am your personal bodyguard and protector."

"Isn't that the same thing?"

"What is your point? I am on double duty." His tone was matter-a-fact and she hoped that, eventually she would be able to take him down a peg or two. Jack was starting to get on her nerves and it was difficult to remember that he could also be Ethan.

Chapter 2

The bridge was wider than Gabby expected. When Jack had called it a bridge, she had imagined one of those one or two people wooden bridges.

This bridge made her think of a Central Park Bridge that a car could easily drive over.

They both stood there in awe at the smooth gray stones and the drop that was hidden by a misty fog. That fog easily covered half of the bridge, obscuring the other side.

"I guess this is your first quest," Jack sighed. "The Forest would do something like this."

"Hush," she hissed. "I'm thinking."

Jack paced back and forth as Gabby pondered this predicament. If he was annoying her then she did not show it.

Looking back and forth between the stone bridge and the forest, Gabby cautiously stated, "The Forest won't let us pass until I identify this story."

"Correct," he curtly answered her, not liking this latest development.

"So, I have to cross the bridge." Gabby paused, "What's the worst that could happen?"

Before she could move in any direction, Jack blocked her. "I have to tell you something."

"Okay?" she cautiously asked him while trying to look past him and at the bridge. Curiosity burned at her and she felt an overwhelming urge to discover what the Forest wanted her to uncover.

While trying to predict her next move, he carefully skirted the information that he dreaded having to tell her. "You cannot cross this bridge. If you get stuck in a time loop, then the Kingdom will suffer."

"I doubt it is that big of a deal." She tried to push forward but Jack blocked her.

"It is. Your mother is ill. Some of the doctors think that she is dying." He repeated what his father had told him before Jack was sent to find and retrieve the princess.

Gabby dropped down in the dirt. "And yet I still have to Quest."

Coldly, as if he disagreed with the Forest's decisions, he answered her with a, "Yes."

Using a tone that was a decent impression of Jack's dry tones, she mumbled, "Great."

After looking at the fog engulfed bridge for several minutes, Gabby took a deep breath. "Come along, Jack. We have a quest to complete. The Forest would not push me into this direction knowing that it could lead to the destruction of its trees."

For a brief moment, the trees trembled in fear before straightening back into place.

"This is not about getting pulled into temptations; this is about resisting and being able to problem-solve." Gabby thought aloud, trying to explain to Jack what this quest was really about. "Stay behind me. I'll walk close enough to be able to identify this island and if I get stuck you will pull me back through."

Jack nodded his head in understanding. His instincts told him to walk in front of her in case there were any creepy three-headed fog monsters that had a taste for monarchs. He also knew that he needed to listen to his leader. It was not an easy position for him since he was used to being the leader himself.

Gabby felt the barrier between the two lands. There was slight hesitance as she pushed through, her body slowly disappearing with each step forward.

"Can you hear me?" she carefully asked Jack, not liking what she was hearing on her own end. A persistent buzzing started forming in her ears and she could scarcely understand his answer.

"Barely. You sound foggy."

It had taken only a few steps past the center of the bridge for Gabby to know what story they were about to enter. "This is *The Giver*, or at least how I always pictured the town, and if we aren't allowed back across the bridge we could be here a while depending on if it's one book or all four books and you made it sound as if my mother doesn't have time to produce another daughter."

Gabby stared longingly at this new world that she was more than tempted to enter. It had been a favorite story of hers for years. She had watched the movie at least ten times, picking out the details that varied from the books and dissecting them as she tried to figure out if it took away or added to the story.

Finally, "Slide your hand through and pull me out," she commanded, hoping he could hear her.

Thankfully his hand slid through the barrier shortly after her order. Gabby clasped Jack's hand and she felt him trying to tug her forward, but his hand and her body would not move. Letting go, she watched as Jack started to swear, his hand stuck between the two stories. The bridge declared that he could only move forward. Finally, he caved and joined her on the story's side.

She warily looked back and forth between the story she'd identified and the barrier preventing their return. "If I already identified the story and we are still on the bridge, do we still have to enter the story?"

"I do not know," Jack answered worriedly. "Why?" He was staring fascinated at the black and white landscape that revealed an occasional glimpse of red. He then mentally added this to the series of questions that had been forming ever since he had learned about the bridges and their various tales.

Carefully she explained, "Because Plan A just failed."

The problem was that the bridge didn't want them to go back across to the Enchanted Forest. They walked right into the barrier that was in the middle of the bridge. No amount of pushing would make the nearly invisible barrier budge. Jack laughed as Gabby recited passwords from as many books and stories that she could remember. When he made some pillows and blankets randomly appear, Gabby was distracted for a moment, asking for explanations and was unsatisfied with his, "Magic is everywhere," explanation.

It wasn't an hour later when Gabby struggled to wake up. The hard stone was finally making itself known underneath the ridiculously soft pillows and blankets. "It's all a dream," she thought.

Yes, it was all a dream. Everything that Ethan Clark told her about being adopted and her having to magically return her to her "real" home because her mother was dying was nothing but a dream; even if the bedding was softer than it should be at home.

That didn't matter. This was a dream. She was at home with her parents: Preston and Michaela Harrington. She was in the middle of Winter Break and that was why her room was so chilly; she had accidentally left her bedroom window open and a cold front had come through. Yes. That had to be the right explanation.

Opening her eyes, the first thing Gabby did was let out a scream.

It wasn't a dream. She wasn't at "home" with her "parents." She was twenty-one years old and facing her first Enchanted Forest trial while standing on a bridge between two not-so-fictional fictional worlds.

Jerking upwards, Jack speedily pulled a dagger out of his boot. "What? Is there a giant three-headed fog monster?"

She could have continued on into that fictional world knowing that she could get "stuck" there and evade her responsibility as the next Queen of Wonderland or she could find a way off of the bridge that held her hostage.

Jack, still worried, unknowingly started acting more like Ethan than his Huntsman counterpart. "What's wrong?"

Ignoring him, Gabby started to think. Even she knew that the easy trials were given first. They were designed to lull the Quester into a false sense of security. It was written into almost every single fairy tale she had ever read. It was

Tradition. Was the Enchanted Forest powered more on Tradition or the tales that broke Traditions?

Without thinking she started hitting Jack as she released her frustration against the questions she couldn't answer. Hitting the bridge would result in broken bones and she suspected that Jack wouldn't stop her.

"Whoa! Wait! It's only me!" Jack grumbled, holding his arms out against her sleepy assault. "Calm down."

"You mean all of this wasn't a dream?" Gabby plopped back down on a blanket and wrapped her arms around herself. "I really am a Wonderland Princess and heir to a throne in a land that I always thought was a fictional children's story. I was adopted when I was two years old and my adoptive parents never felt the need to tell me that someday I would vanish in a puff of smoke…"

"We did not disappear in a puff of smoke. Only Caterpillars do that," Jack interrupted, settling down next to her but not touching the Princess in fear of what she would unleash next.

Ignoring him, Gabby continued with her rant. "…leaving my identity behind with everything that I ever thought was fact or fiction. My biological family is waiting for me and my biological mother is apparently dying and I might miss her while I'm on this quest because I'm stranded on a bridge that refuses to let me pass because of some stupid idea that I have to get sucked into a story that I already know and have identified. Who knows how long I'll be stuck here when I should be completing my quest and spending time with my dying mother. Why can't this be a dream?"

"I am afraid it is not." While he was looking at her, he missed what was happening behind them.

"What?" Gabby asked, jerking backward as if noticing that Jack was there for the first time since her rambling tirade began. This caused her to fall backward and through the barrier that she was leaning against. "The barrier is gone," she whispered, stunned.

"Then let us get out of here before it decides to reform." With a snap of his fingers, Jack made all of the bedding disappear as they hurried back to the seemingly never-ending forest side of the bridge.

"Can you bring those blankets and pillows so that we can get back to sleep?" Gabby asked when they were firmly on solid ground. They couldn't see the path in the dark and all she wanted to do was go back to sleep after the exhaustive verbal purge that did very little to calm her ragged emotions.

Grinning, he took the opportunity to try to show her a little about what she was capable of doing. "You could try it yourself."

"Maybe later," she yawned as a pillow appeared in her arms. Gabby was tired enough to not realize that she'd summoned the pillow herself.

Jack stayed awake a little while longer as he tried to figure out what it was the Princess had said that had caused the barrier to vanish. Finally giving up, he summoned his own pillow and blanket, tucked the dagger underneath the bedding, and fell into a restless sleep. He was her protector and needed to remain on guard.

Chapter 3

They had been walking aimlessly for days when out of nowhere a gingerbread house appeared. There were a few crumbling edges and they could see where hungry children had taken to breaking and biting into the walls and candies decorating the outside. Melted sugar was crafted into a kaleidoscope window. Easily overlooked was the small sign beside the gate of a candy cane fence.

"How does this house not dissolve when it rains?" Gabby questioned, looking around at everything including the candied apples that were hanging from the trees.

Jack answered her simply with one word, "Magic."

"Of course," she rolled her eyes in response.

The small sign read 'Hansel and Gretel's Old-Fashioned Candy Shoppe' and was easily hidden by cotton candy shaped into flowers. "They must not want to do much business," Gabby idly remarked while tapping on the sign as they entered the fence.

Rolling his eyes, Jack carefully explained, "Hansel and Gretel's is a well-established local shop. People come from the surrounding kingdoms just for a chance at getting some of their homemade fudge and freshly baked gingerbread houses. Not everything can be judged based on appearances."

Looking up at the house that was bigger than she expected it to be, Gabby wondered about their story. How many generations had run this particular shop? Why did they decide to stick around where they were almost cooked alive?

Jack knew that it was time to explain this story to her. His recent visit let him know that The Brothers Grimm had not gotten every part of this story right. Leading Gabby to the rock candy bench, he started with parts of the story he doubted she knew. "Hansel and Gretel were sent out into the woods by their father and step-mother. The step-mother, pregnant with the woodcutter's third child, never expected the children to return night after night, arms full of whatever errand they had been sent out on. One night she slipped out to speak to the local witch. The tales about this woman's abilities and dietary preferences were far-reaching, but it never bothered the locals. Whenever a family was too poor to feed all of their children, they would send away the weakest child so that there would be more food around the table. Hansel and Gretel had no choice; their step-mother knew that she could not get rid of one without the other."

Taking a deep breath, Jack continued with the story; it was the first time that he'd ever had to regale anybody with this particular story. "That night she made a bargain with the witch; two children in exchange for her husband's circumstances to improve. Once their deal was made, the step-mother returned to her home, unaware that Hansel had been following her for the entire trip. That night he searched the house for anything he could use as a guide to help them return home, but all he could find was the bread meant for that morning's breakfast. The rest you already know. "

"But," Gabby interrupted, "that doesn't tell me how they gained the cottage."

Snorting, Jack let down his guard for a moment and used a tone Gabby frequently recognized from her time sitting in class next to Ethan, "You have not let me finish."

"Sorry." She knew that she needed to work on her impatience.

"Once the witch was cooked in the oven and turned into gingerbread, several other children reappeared from the walls and other places she had used gingerbread children instead of eating them. Among the children were several of their playmates and friends. Hansel had already carefully explained to Gretel about their step-mother's plans and the other children in the cottage had heard his tale. They all decided to stay, including the baker's youngest daughter who knew how to bake treats without children in them. Agatha and Meino ended up staying the longest, eventually marrying Hansel and Gretel. Our current proprietors are Mina and Tavin. They are married, but Tavin adopted some orphans from a Scandinavian orphanage; we have liaisons throughout the world that make dual world adoptions possible."

Right then somebody calling for "Erich" and "Annaliese" echoed through the trees. "Time for dinner!" the feminine voice sounded.

Nearby the sound of shrieks and "Five more minutes" bounced from tree to tree.

"No, now, and bring our guests with you," a masculine tone commanded.

Looking up at Jack, Gabby's eyes reflected her question. "They have cameras," Jack explained, pointing towards one of the corner eves, "to defer anybody from eating the walls and windows."

Nodding her head, Gabby stood and shook out her cloak. It was no longer the bright red that it had been only a few days before, but her heritage was still clear. "Will they know that I'm also Wonderlandian?"

"Not unless you want to tell them," Jack answered.

Pausing for a long moment, "I don't want to tell them unless I have to, but I think that the tiny blue spade on your necklace will tell them for me."

Jack looked down at the necklace he had long forgotten he was wearing: the universal signal for a royal family member's bodyguard. Anybody who recognized it would know that Jack was guarding a member of Wonderland's royal family. Slipping it into his shirt, he grinning and looked at her before asking, "Better?"

"Much."

Mina had a secret. She had not gone through hell and back in order for some upstart royal to recognize her. Pamina, the daughter of the Sun and Moon had hidden away from her betrothed and parents, ever hopeful that being in a different realm and hidden among the trees would help hide her from their ever-watchful gaze. She had not gone through hell only to lose Tamino five years later.

She did know how much Tavin knew about her; just that they had found each other in The Enchanted Forest and that she had two different colored eyes: silver and gold. But what she did not know was eclipsed by what she did know.

"Good evening, Your Majesty, Her Majesty's protector," she greeted her guests. Ignoring Gabby's look of shock, she led everybody into the cottage.

She had paid Hansel and Gretel's remaining descendant into letting her manage the Old-Fashioned Candy Shoppe until Gretel could find somebody to help her carry on her family name. The other girl had been gone for five years now. Tavin never knew the truth.

Looking closely, she knew where there were still faint imprints of gingerbread children on the walls. Mina cared to not think about the knife marks scoring the wooden table in the middle of the kitchen.

"How did you know?" Gabby whispered from behind her.

Turning with her unsettling gaze, Mina met Gabby's blue stare, "I know far more than I care to reveal."

Gabby nodded her head, "I understand, Pamina," was all she said.

"How?" Mina whispered, ignoring the shocked look on the Huntsman's face. "Nobody else has ever caught that."

"It was my adoptive parents' favorite opera and I ended up devouring any retelling I could get my hands on. There aren't many, but there was enough."

Panicked, Mina looked around the room before leaning forward and whispering, "Don't tell Tavin; he doesn't know."

Curiosity once again overtook her and Gabby didn't resist the urge to ask, "And the orphans?"

Letting out a bone-deep sigh, Mina confided in the Princess. She doubted that a royal trying to hide underneath a red cloak would reveal any of the candy maker's secrets.

"They are the children I had with Tamino; my mother forced me to leave them behind by kidnapping them and depositing them at the orphanage shortly after Tamino's death. She thought they would be too much of a distraction with their brown eyes and brown hair. I think Mother was angry that neither child took after me."

Shouting from outside told the trio that Tavin and the children were about to return.

Tilting her head, Gabby examined the woman sitting beside her. Something was not quite right about her appearance. Suddenly it occurred to her and she whispered, "But your hair?"

Leaning forward, Mina shared a secret that would prove useful later. "I dye it using coffee or tea."

Nodding her head, Gabby considered what she knew about natural hair dyes, which wasn't much. "Clever."

"What is going on?" Jack finally interjected, not liking how the woman was starting to lean in towards each other and whispering things that he could not hear.

Turning to look at her bodyguard, Gabby quickly explained, "The Enchanted Forest has a refugee." Turning to Mina, "If you ever need a more secure location, I believe

I'm within my rights to give you protection in Wonderland if you never need it."

Jack tilted his head while he pondered her offer. It made him wonder just how much of a benevolent ruler the Princess would make.

Three bodies, one tall and two short, came tumbling into the kitchen. They could see that the little girl had grabbed a handful of candy and was stuffing it into her dress pocket. Without a word, Mina reached into the pocket and pulled out the colorful candy. "You can get it back after dinner. Now, Erich, Annaliese, say hello to our guests, Jack and Gabby."

"Hello," the siblings greeted the travelers with a long look. Annaliese even bobbed a slight curtsy before sliding into her seat.

"Hello," Jack and Gabby answered them, smiles carefully painted on their faces.

"You must stay for dinner and later we'll insist on you taking some provisions for your long journey. There is no telling how long the Forest will keep you wandering." Tavin slipped into his own seat while making his offer.

"Thank you very much," Jack accepted. "Sometimes it gets quite difficult to shoot our own dinner if the Forest does not allow it." He remembered how many times he had seen Talking Animals disappear into the trees moments after he realized exactly what he was aiming his bow towards.

Chapter 9

Several more days passed without anything important happening. Gabby would catch the occasional glimpse of a castle through the trees. Jack explained the differences between her world and this world. When his habit of drilling her over the proper way to address people in various stations of life became tedious – often Gabby wished another bridge would appear so that she could toss him over the side of it – they switched to discussing some of the reading assignments from the classes that they had shared or she would share stories about the bridges they would pass.

It was easy to not pay attention to the time or where they were going because the Forest was directing them in the direction it wanted them to go anyway. Most of their time was spent debating things that had been happened in their English classes. Jack had wanted to know more about some of their readings, having never actually done any research for any of the papers that they had been required to write.

"How did you get away with that?" Gabby finally got up the nerve to ask him one day.

"I was auditing the classes. Nobody seemed to notice that I was auditing every single class that I was taking. That way I could still sit in on the lectures. but never had to do any of the necessary essays or papers." Jack looked pleased with himself at being able to get away with using what he considered a small amount of magic in the non-magical world.

Gabby simply shook her head in disbelief. "At least you did some of the readings. I still remember how stunned Dr. Prescott was when you stated that Grendel was mad about not being allowed to live at Hrothgar's hall because he was a monster."

The memory still left him confused. He had trouble chalking up the different interpretations to the different lifestyle he had lived compared to his classmates. "I do not know why so many people were terrified of Grendel. They could have stood up against him if they wanted to. Was there ever any proof that he was a monster...?"

"Well…" Gabby raked her memory, "he was eating them…"

"And...?" he asked her as if it didn't change his opinion.

Shaking her head, Gabby described what she remembered from her high school class when they had discussed the story. "Grendel would tear them apart limb for limb and could easily decimate the kingdom."

"Then Hrothgar should have destroyed him." Everything was black and white to the Huntsman and all he could think was that the King should have protected and fought for his people, even if it meant rushing towards his own death.

"He couldn't. It would have left his kingdom defenseless when Grendel destroyed him," Gabby paused as she happened to see something moving up ahead. It would be the first time they would encounter something besides trees and the occasional bird or talking animal. "Besides I always pictured him with a tail." Before Jack could say anything else, she continued, "But you come from a place where animals can talk and monsters really do exist."

Looking ahead, she saw that unidentified something she'd spotted moving on the side of the road. "Does this place have dragons?" Gabby asked carefully, stating the first mythological creature she could think of that also matched the description of the creature she saw ahead of them on the road.

Eying the Princess carefully, Jack wondered about her change of topic. "Nobody has ever seen one, but anybody who has ever gone hunting for one has never been seen again."

"That probably means that there are dragons." Nodding her head, Gabby started to wonder what they should do about the upcoming challenge. She suspected that Jack had yet to see the dragon about a hundred meters in front of them.

"I doubt it. Everybody knows that 'I'm hunting dragons is code for…'" he trailed off as soon as he caught a glimpse of what she had spotted. He then kicked himself for being so unobservant.

"Code for what?" Gabby asked before noticing that Jack had stopped in his tracks. "That the head of the household was abandoning his family?" she continued, wanting to finish her thoughts more than anything else. She was amazed that with as alert as he'd been throughout their journey that it took him so long to notice what she'd observed minutes before.

On the path in front of them was a shiny blue-green - Gabby argued later that it was turquoise - baby dragon the size of a horse.

Trying to keep the smug tone out of her voice and failing, she turned to watch him. "You were saying?"

They stared at each other and at the creature in front of them. Jack was more shocked than anything because he had never seen a dragon before. It was the last thing that he ever imagined he would encounter. He really did think that they were made up excuses for a father abandoning his family after his wife died or when he made a regrettable match. Gabby was wondering why the dragon was shaking and not breathing fire at them. The dragon was standing there shaking and wondering when they were going to attack with swords.

"So, what am I going to do about this dragon, Oh Mighty Huntsman?"

"I...don't...know," Jack froze, staring at the little wyrmling and wondering where its parents were.

Surprised that Jack didn't have a clue about what to do; she hesitated in asking, "Am I supposed to slay it?"

Until that moment the dragon had been looking back and forth between the two humans. They were dressed funny; the human girl was not wearing a skirt and both were wearing these weird blue pants. "Slay me? You mean...kill me," she squeaked. "Mam and Pap warned me about this.

They told me that if any human saw me they would want to kill me. Humans always want to kill dragons," she wailed.

Gabby and Jack stared amazed as the little horse-sized dragon stood shaking in the middle of the path. That was when Gabby noticed that one of the dragon's wings was bent awkwardly.

"Why won't she fly away," Jack asked, not really paying as much attention to the dragon as Gabby thought he should be doing.

"She can't. Something is wrong with her wing." Gabby paused as she observed the scene carefully.

"She?"

Rolling her eyes, Gabby replied, "Her voice is high pitched."

"Oh." He still looked stunned and it didn't help that the Princess acted as if she already had a plan.

"Will you please quit talking about my poor wing and kill me already," the wyrmling shook. The tear that rolled down her snout nearly broke Gabby's heart.

Taking a step forward, the Princess cautiously asked, "What is wrong with your wing?"

As she approached the dragon, Jack noticed that the only path that remained was the tiny patch that they were standing on. It appeared that the little wyrmling noticed too since she started to shake even more.

"Oh no, oh no," she repeated. "I'm a quest. I'm part of somebody's quest. Who? Who is going to kill me? Which one of you has the pleasure to kill a poor, defenseless, and injured dragon in a quest to assure their little patch of the world that they are worthy of sitting upon a blasted throne?" The dragon looked back and forth between Jack and Gabby. "It's you, isn't it," she asked Jack. "You look like you wouldn't know what to do with a dragon if you crossed paths with one. In this case me!"

"Actually, that would be me," Gabby whispered, looking at the wing. "Did you go through a briar patch, by chance?"

Shaking, "Yes, I did. I was playing with Windy and he flew into me and knocked me down. I couldn't get my bearings, I am only a hundred years old and a bit clumsy after all, and tumbled down to earth. When I landed, I managed to roll – I did remember to do that at least – but I rolled right into this area with these thorns and my wing took the most damage." Turning her head to look at where Gabby stood, the dragon whispered, "Are you going to kill me now?"

Looking at the thorns and torn membrane, Gabby glanced up, "Why would I kill you? You haven't done anything to us."

"Yet," Jack mumbled.

Hush." The Princess scolded him before turning back to the dragon and questioning her, "Why didn't you flame at us or anything? I get why you didn't fly away." Pausing, "Hold still for a few minutes, this might hurt."

"What are you doing?" The dragon smiled when Gabby jerked her head up as soon as she realized that the wyrmling had turned her head and neck to where she could see what Gabby was doing.

"I'm removing the thorns. I don't know how else to fix your torn wing." Carefully removing a thorn, she repeated her previous question, "Now, why didn't you flame at us?"

Shaking her head and long neck sadly as if the humans before her were idiots, the dragon huffed at them, "I told you already; I'm only a hundred years old. A hundred and three to be exact. Dragons don't learn how to flame until they are fully grown and I have about forty-seven more years to go before that happens."

Gabby's eyes went wide. "That quickly? How big do dragons get?"

The dragon looked over at Jack for help. "Don't look at me. I've never seen a fully-grown dragon before," he shook his head. Instead, he moved over to the injured wing to help Gabby pick out thorns.

"I'm somewhere between a fifth and a fourth the size of my parents, depending on which parent you are comparing me to. I'll probably be smaller than my Pap because my Mam is smaller and I'm a girl."

"What is your name?"

"Sea Foam," the wyrmling proudly proclaimed. "Mam says I am the color of the sea and she teases Pap about playing in the foam."

"That is a very pretty name. I am Gabby."

Jack rolled his eyes, a very un-Jack-like action. "This is Her Royal Highness Princess Gabrielle of Wonderland," he corrected Gabby's informal introduction.

Gabby chuckled as the dragon's eyes grew in size, making her look like an oversized puppy dog. "A princess? A real-life princess? I've always wanted to meet a princess. Nobody is going to believe that a princess helped me with my wing," the wyrmling rambled as she lowered her head in a bow. "It's a pleasure, Princess."

"Gabby," the Princess interrupted. "Please, call me Gabby."

"Princess Gabby," the dragon sighed with pleasure, still bowing. "I'm on casual terms with a Princess. This is the second-best day of my life!"

"Look up," Gabby commanded. "No, Sea Foam, just call me Gabby. I was not raised here; I am not used to being a princess quite yet. Until we get to Wonderland, I am just Gabby."

"Can I join you?" Sea Foam grinned. "I can't fly for a few more days until my wings completely heal, but I can look big and intimidating if anything tries to attack you." She looked over Jack as if he was incapable of doing the job. She'd seen the way he had frozen up when he'd first see her.

Pulling her aside, Jack tried to argue with her about the safety of allowing a growing dragon to join them on her quest.

The only thing that Gabby had to say in response to his protests was, "Don't ever say that something is unlikely or won't happen or doesn't exist again! Every single time you have the forest has thrown one directly into our path!"

Gabby sped up, not caring how much distance she put between Jack and herself. In fact, at the moment the more space between them the better. He had thoroughly annoyed her in his attempts to persuade her to leave the wyrmling behind.

"What did I do?" Jack asked Sea Foam the Dragon.

"She grumbling about 'idiotic men' so it's probably because you are a men," Sea Foam answered. Jack did not bother to correct her grammar.

Chapter 5

What appeared to be hidden deep in the woods, was actually really a ten-minute walk from the small town of Baerville, was a restaurant. The Enchanted Forest didn't have many restaurants; most people opted to cook at home unless they lived in the bigger towns closer to the castles. The smaller towns mostly had taverns for travelers and people that had been working late. But this restaurant was different.

In one corner was a set of chairs around a table with three empty bowls. Nobody dared touch that historic display. It had sat there for generations undisturbed.

"Are we in..?" Gabby's question trailed off.

"Welcome to the Three Golden Bears Restaurant and Gift Shop!" a perky voice underneath a wig of golden corkscrew curls greeted them. "How many?"

Looking over at Jack, Gabby wondered if they had any money to pay for dinner. The provisions Mina had provided them had lasted for several days, and Sea Foam had proven adept at scanning the land for non-talking animals, but this duo couldn't stomach any more rabbit.

"Are small dragons allowed?" Jack asked while Sea Foam tried to make herself as tiny as possible.

"Of course!" the perky hostess exclaimed. "I'll just take you to the back patio. Your dragonet can go around the house. There's a walking path she can follow. One goes into the woods and leads to the original Baer's cabin, but if you turn right at the corner of the restaurant, you'll find the patio easily enough."

Sea Foam bowed her head before thanking the hostess and disappearing around the side of the building.

Leading the way, the hostess started to chatter, "Are you new to Baerville?"

"Yes," Jack answered. "We're just passing through on our way to…"

"Let me guess," she interrupted, eyeing Jack and Gabby while she made up her mind. "You are a Huntsman and you are leading the Princess to…" she paused to think, "…to Roschen."

Letting out a chuckle, "Close, but not quite," before leaving it at that. Jack had already determined that this hostess was a gossip fishing for more information to spread.

Once the bewigged girl was out of earshot, Gabby leaned closer to Jack and asked, "Roschen?"

"Sleeping Beauty's Kingdom. Most of the Enchanted Forest Kingdoms are named after a characteristic of the tale in the original language or in the language that the tale was most popularly told in. Roschen is German for rose or little rose." Jack didn't look at her once while he was explaining it. "A lot of names you will find can be translated from German."

"Where are we now?"

Jack looked around her as if she was missing something important.

"Look, I know exactly where we are, but I was wondering if we were in a certain kingdom," Gabby huffed, moving to catch up with their hostess before they were lost among the tables.

Looking after her, Jack lengthened his stride in order to catch up. "Honestly, I don't know what kingdom we are in," he finally answered. "Hansel and Gretel's Candy Shoppe was part of Roschen, even though it is on the outskirts of the boundary. This particular kingdom's name has been long forgotten, just like the location of its castle. Most people live near the boundary lines, but there are a lot of talking animals around here. I think Little Red Riding Hood's Grandmother's cottage is somewhere nearby. Normally I would not take you on this route, but the Forest is insisting that we have to pass by here in order to get to Wonderland."

Settling into the chair that Jack had pulled out for her, Gabby looked at the spot where Sea Foam had claimed and curled up into a tight little ball. Somehow the little dragon was able to make the ground look comfortable.

There was a plethora of information that she had to take in and she had a feeling that as soon as she returned to Wonderland that there would be geography lessons on top of etiquette and who knew what else.

"Tell me about this tale," Gabby whispered, hoping that nobody else heard her.

"There are a few versions," Jack started. "One has an old woman and two have Goldilocks. One has three bachelor bears and another has a family of bears. You are most likely to recognize the Papa, Mama, and Baby Bear version. Reality is, this story, like most other tales, have German origins, even though the most popular version is from the United Kingdom, the Baers were actually Adelard, Baldemar, and Carl. They were not actually bears, but with this part of the kingdom, anything could happen. Goldilocks did break into their house, after her older brothers had played a trick on her and had gotten the sixteen-year-old lost in the woods. She saw the Baer's cottage and decided it was the perfect place to rest. She ate Baldemar's porridge, broke Carl's chair, and fell asleep in Adelard's bed. Once the Baers found her asleep, they puzzled over what to do. Adelard was all for keeping her and Carl thought she'd make a perfect housekeeper. It was Baldemar who scared her and caused her to run away."

"Oh," their server smiled as she interrupted their story. She wore bear ears on her head. "You know the real story!"

Jack turned red as the girl continued to praise him. "It is part of my job knowing this Forest's tales."

"Then you must be a Huntsman," the server gushed, touching his arm flirtatiously. "I've always wanted to meet a Huntsman." Smiling widely, "I'm Heather."

Gabby could feel a flash of jealousy in the pit of her stomach as she watched Heather running her hand up and down Jacks' bicep. From the doorway, a male voice sounded, "Heather, you are supposed to take orders and not flirt with other girls' significant others." It still didn't ease her ruffled feathers as Heather apologized, backed away, and went back to pretending to be professional.

"I am Jack Huntsman and this is Princess Gabrielle of Wonderland," Jack said coolly, annoyed that their server was more consumed with flirting with him instead of doing her job. He, more than anybody, knew the importance of doing the job a person was tasked with doing and the weeks it was taking to return the Princess to her home was wearing his patience thin.

The Princess and Seafoam both held back laughter as Heather froze in place. The Kingdoms were aware that it was nearing time for the Wonderland Princess to return. Even the table next to them froze in place as they wondered what Heather and the Princess would do next. It was extremely apparent to the entire patio that Heather had been rude to the Princess.

"Your Majesty," Heather curtsied, hiding the fact that she was unable to make eye contact and her face had turned red with shame. "My apologies for being inappropriate towards your bodyguard."

Smiling benignly, Gabby looked at the young girl, "No apologies necessary."

Straightening her spine, the waitress returned to her duties by asking, "What can I get you to drink?"

Looking at Jack, she allowed him to place their order. Within moments, their server had disappeared and she gestured to him to continue with his story. "What happened next?"

Grinning at her, he felt the need to compliment her ability before continuing, "You handled that superbly."

"Thank you. Now, what happened to Goldilocks?" Gabby was eager to learn the variations to the familiar tales she had grown up reading.

Shaking his head, "Two years passed and Goldilocks found herself once again near the Baer's cabin. Carl was out back taking care of his garden. Baldemar was in town getting supplies; nobody was willing to double-cross or offer him a bad deal. However, Adelard was sitting on the front porch thinking about what piece of furniture he was going to work on next. While he was thinking about crafting tables and chairs, Goldilocks wandered up, sat down next to him, and they started talking. A year later they were married. Adelard ended up building her this house so that they did not have to share space with Baldemar and Carl, especially when Goldilocks revealed that she was expecting his child."

Releasing a sigh, Gabby stared at the wall behind Jack's head. "I swear sometimes you are not a cold-hearted Jack. How can you be anything but an Ethan when you can tell me stories like this?"

"I am doing my duty as a Card and a Huntsman. It is my job to know these stories."

Sighing, Gabby picked up her drink to bite back the comments she was tempted to make.

Chapter 6

The last thing either of them expected to appear out of nowhere was a tower. Easily over seventy feet tall, the base was wider than the path and a hedge of briar thorns circled the smooth stones.

"Always briars," Gabby mumbled, wondering idly how many tales used thorn bushes as a deterrent.

Without a second thought, Jack shouted, "Rapunzel, Rapunzel, let down your golden hair!"

Shaking her head, Gabby snorted when nothing happened. "You are too late, Ethan." Pointing out their thorny obstacle, she reminded him, "The witch cast the thorns after cutting off Rapunzel's hair. She then used the hair to trap and blind the prince."

Jack laughed. "My fair princess, no witch except Rapunzel herself cast the briar thorn hedge. In fact, she was the one who tricked the witch before pushing her over the balcony and into the thorns."

Gabby turned to face him. "What? No happily ever after?"

"The prince was the one who cut her hair."

Looking up at the tower blocking their path, Gabby thought about the changes to all the fairy tales that Ethan had told her. Nothing ever was as it appeared to be and that seemed to the lesson that the Forest was attempting to make certain she learned.

"Well, we still have to get around this tower somehow," she remarked while looking around the base for a clue. A faint trail appeared and waving towards him, she started down the path.

Jack, because he was acting more like Jack than he was acting like a friend at the moment, didn't notice the darkening skies until it was too late. Maybe it was the trees or the tower blocking him from clearly seeing the storm clouds brewing. Maybe he was angry with himself for his growing feelings for Gabby.

He had tried to ignore them in college as he watched her around her friends, magically manipulated potential suitors from her path, and tried to ignore his growing fascination with her smile.

Tried and failed. Not that he could ever let her know that.

She was Wonderland Royalty and destined to become a Queen. And he was Jack Huntsman and destined to guard her and the kingdoms.

It was not in the stars.

"Umm…" Gabby hesitated, "are those storm clouds approaching?" She looked up toward the sky as she noticed that everything around them started to darken.

Looking up, he shouted, "Run!" just as the skies opened up, dousing them with a cold, wet stream of rain that made it nearly impossible for them to see the Granny's Cottage ahead.

Nearly impossible. It was almost as if the Forest wanted them to see the cottage and take refuge within its walls. Running into Rapunzel's tower and discovering the faint trail had not been an accident.

Running inside and trying not to slide across the floors, Jack saw Sea Foam disappear into a small stable – she wouldn't be able to fit through the cottage door – before closing the door against the storm.

"All we need is some light and then I'll start a fire," Jack stated as he listened to Gabby's teeth chattering as the cold started to make itself felt.

"That will not be necessary," a voice coldly behind him stated before hitting Jack on the back of the head with a book and pouncing on Gabby before Jack had even fallen to the floor.

Within moments Gabby found herself bound to a chair as the cloaked figure stroked the fire. Unable to move, she watched him drag Ethan down the cellar stairs and into the darkness below, leaving her alone on the main floor of the building.

"If this is a quest," she whispered to the walls around her, "then it better be my last one because I have no intention of becoming somebody's meal."

She could recognize the basic bones of a tale without having to think about it. She suspected that it was bound to happen the moment they landed in the Enchanted Forest. She still wore the red cloak around her body; the material had helped keep the rough rope from cutting into her arms where the…man…had secured her to the chair.

Gabby suspected that he was originally a Huntsman; his cloak matched the one that Jack wore. What he was now was a mystery.

Jack opened his eyes and groaned as he felt the pounding in his head and the knot on the back of it. "They should take my Huntsman cloak away from me for letting that monster knock me out."

Listening to the air around him, he expected to hear Gabby's breathing. Maybe she was still knocked unconscious. She had to be in the cellar with him. It was unthinkable that the Princess could be anywhere else. "Gabby?"

Feeling around the floor he found a chair that was wrapped in a rope and something he wished that he could not identify. Next was the stack of crates against the wall. This helped him up where his head found itself lost in a sea of cloaks that were hanging from the rafters.

Holding his breath, he carefully felt around them, hoping that it was nothing but cloaks hanging around. Hoping it was not like the skeleton he had found still tied to the chair. Slowly, carefully, he started to count them.

"One…two…three…four…ten...eleven…twelve…twenty-five…twenty-six…twenty-seven…"

Finally, he found the stairs and the cellar door. Without thinking about it he started pounding on the door in an attempt at breaking it down. He had to save Gabby.

Gabby stared at the rattling cellar door behind the odd hybrid of wolf and Huntsman. What was that creature? Furry ears and a human face that was shaped like a furless snout? Human hands that ended in claws? Human calves that looked like the hind legs of a werewolf? Was he a Wolf-Huntsman? Wolfman? Were-Huntsman?

The bigger question was – were there more like him? The potential answer terrified her.

"Princess," he snarled, "your bodyguard cannot protect you this time." The door behind him continued to shake, but the wooden bar across the frame prevented the door from opening. "And if your pet dragon comes in, she will destroy this entire place." A growl was heard from a window.

Pretending to be unruffled, Gabby gawked at him straight on while she summoned the courage to ask, "Who are you?"

"Do you not mean, 'What am I'?"

Shrugging her shoulders to the best of her ability, she countered with, "Does it matter?"

Chuckling his growly laugh, he moved to stand in front of her. "Not really. I am Howard. I was the weakest of my fellow Huntsmen, but as the second son of a minor nobleman I had little choice in the matter of careers."

Shaking his head as he paused, he waited long enough to see if the Princess would make any comments. Hearing nothing, he continued, "One night I was on guard duty when a wolf attacked me. For some reason, I became this."

"Was it a full moon?" Gabby whispered, the question slipping out before she could stop it.

Allowing his tone to reveal that he was impressed with her question, he grinned before answering her, "Yes, it was."

Gabby searched her mind for werewolf lore as Howard continued to talk, telling her about his hatred for Huntsmen, how he was bullied because of his small stature until he changed forms and killed his tormentors. He told her about his dislike of anybody and everybody connected to the Red Riding Hood line. How he uses an abandoned Granny's Cottage to lure the red hoods in and cooked them Gingerbread Witch style.

Once again chuckling, Howard started to reveal his plans. There was nothing for him to worry about at this point. The Princess was tied to a chair and her protector was locked in the basement with his food source. "You, my Princess, I shall eat raw. I will make your dragon and Huntsman watch while I tear out your heart…"

All Howard heard was the increased rattle of the door behind him as Gabby thrust a silver dinner knife into his heart.

Backing away, she started sobbing as Howard collapsed onto the wooden planks in front of her, staring motionless at the silver knife sticking out of his chest. Gabby remained standing there sobbing, staring, and shaking until Ethan's shouting caught her attention.

Somehow, he had managed to escape the cellar and when saying her name in normal tones did nothing to rouse her from a stunned stupor, he started getting louder and louder until it worked.

"I thought he'd…" Ethan whispered as he hugged her tightly, leading her towards the outside door. "It was you or him and we need you more than somebody who has killed at least twenty red-hooded girls." She did not need to know that he was downplaying the number of red-hoods that were in that cellar.

"How," she hiccupped, "do you know that?"

"He kept the cloaks as trophies hanging around in the cellar." Once again, he downplayed his discoveries.

It was still the wrong thing to say as Gabby started sobbing harder than before. Carrying her the rest of the way outside, he walked several yards into the woods until the house vanished from sight. It was a risky move to leave the path, but all Ethan could think was that he needed to get her away from that house.

As she started to retch into the bushes, losing all of the meager breakfast they had eaten that morning, Ethan stroked her hair back and tried his best to comfort her. Right then, at that very moment, he was more her friend than he was her bodyguard.

Pulling her towards him, Ethan did the only thing he could think of doing. The only thing he had been thinking about doing for hours since they escaped Granny's Cottage. Pushing stray strands of hair from her face, he leaned down and kissed her.

He had waited until she had calmed down, resisting the urge he felt knowing it could scare her.

Going slowly, he gave Gabby the chance to pull away from him and was surprised when she bridged the gap between the two of them. Her boldness caused him to freeze for a moment before pressing his lips against hers. Without asking, her mouth opened, inviting him in and not letting him back away from the kiss.

"About time!" Sea Foam huffed before noisily clomping back into the bushes.

Pulling apart, Gabby leaned her head against his chest as she tried to calm down her breathing. "Seriously though, Ethan." Closing her eyes, she replayed the scene in her head a little bit longer, wreaking havoc on her attempts to get her breathing and heartbeat back under control.

Taking a step backward and breaking their connection, Jack began apologizing, "I'm so sorry, Princess. I overstepped my bounds."

Looking up at him, she wondered what she was going to say to him. Instead, she started marching forward. She'd leave her thoughts in her head for a while longer until she had some coherent statement about how his sense of duty was misplaced sometimes.

Chapter 7

A few days after the event with the Were-Huntsman that Gabby refused to talk about and the event that had her scratching her head in confusion, they stumbled on some interesting footprints. The weird prints on the path had the trio scratching their heads. They were not dragon footprints – Seafoam was able to compare her foot to the print. Gabby thought that it was a giant chicken print. Only, why would there be a giant chicken in the Enchanted Forest?

Uncertain how to address him after their kiss, she whispered cautiously, "Umm…Ethan?"

"Yes?" he quickly answered her. He was incapable of keeping his emotions out of his voice; it was tinted with confusion and the other emotions he refused to address but refused to stay buried.

"Why would the Enchanted Forest have a giant chicken?" Still, not looking at him, she studied the impression carefully, hoping that she was wrong.

Ethan turned to look at Gabby with horror slightly etched into his expression. "Giant Chicken?"

Blue eyes met hazel for one of the few times since he had pulled away from her. "That's what the print looks like," Gabby pointed out.

Drawing out his sword, he looked around the clearing. The threat was imminent. He just had to find it. There was a slim chance that this new development was not as dangerous as he feared. The Princess had encountered her three Enchanted Forest trials, so why would the Forest toss her towards this possible danger?

"Get between me and Seafoam," he commanded, not looking at her.

Stubbornly Gabby refused to move while she challenged his demand with a simple question. "Why?"

This time he made eye contact when he answered her. "Because I said so."

It was the wrong thing to say. Gabby moved to stand in front of him. "No. Not until you tell me why." She didn't care how serious he was – serious enough to make eye contact with her – because she was just that annoyed with him.

"Baba Yaga," was all that Jack said in response.

"What?" She asked, stepping backward. She didn't move away because she had never heard or read about Baba Yaga; she moved away because she wasn't expecting a Baba Yaga in the Forest. Later she would realize that not expecting a fairy tale just because it wasn't a popular tale didn't mean that it couldn't manifest itself into the Enchanted Forest.

Ethan, channeling his inner Jack, maneuvered Gabby back where he wanted her, before returning to scan the area. "A Baba Yaga has many stories. She is one of the dark sides of the fairy tales. I believe she can be from the Russian or Scandinavian tales. Slavic? Definitely Russian."

Pausing, he noticed the fence about a hundred yards away. "Roughly translated, Baba Yaga means Old Mother, but sometimes when she is spotted, she can be younger or older but that is the thing about magic. Because there are several different tales surrounding her there are different Baba Yaga's of various origins within the Forest. None of them stay in one place. None of them have the same personalities. One tale has three Baba Yagas who are sisters. Some are helpful. Some would eat you rather than help you. In one tale Baba Yaga has to answer the first question that you ever ask her truthfully. In another tale, she helped a Cinderella type of girl but the girl had to perform three extremely difficult tasks."

He wondered if they should approach the gate or if the Forest would let them walk past without any trouble. "If we could see her, we would know which Baba Yaga is nearby. The ones we want to avoid would be holding a broom, mop, or mortar and pestle. They all have a house that can move around because it is on top of chicken legs. Sometimes the house rests on the ground and sometimes the chicken legs do not 'disappear' and the house rests on top of the visible legs. The house is surrounded by a fence made from human bones."

Letting that sink in, Ethan continued in his role of protecting Gabby. He did not expect her to spot the fence and take off towards it.

"What are you doing?"

Turning to face him, Gabby started talking, "Look, Ethan. Maybe I should call you Jack right not because you are acting like a bodyguard and not like my friend." Pausing, "Look, Jack, I've already faced my three Enchanted Forest Trials. Sure, we cannot guarantee what Wonderland is going to give me, but the Forest is not about to send me off to face any more dangers until it deposits me at the

Wonderland Bridge. Now, I am going to think carefully about the wording of my question. I suggest you do the same."

She stopped at the fence, a skull turning to look at her. "May I ask who is calling?" asked the skull.

"I am Gabby Harrington," she hesitated. "I think."

"You are not sure?"

"I am a Quester. My mother is the current Queen of Wonderland. My adopted parents had the last name of Harrington and my bodyguard, Jack, also known as Ethan, has not told me if I have a different last name."

If the skull on the post could nod its head, Gabby thought that this one would. "Do you have a question for the Baba Yaga?"

"Yes, but I don't have it worded in my head yet."

"And do you, Jack Ethan?"

Jack glanced over at Gabby. "I do have a question, but I do not want to know the answer to it."

"Fair enough." Turning to face Gabby once more, the skull advised her to take a moment to think about her question. "The Baba Yaga is not currently in the cottage at the moment anyway. Her cat has gone to locate her and let her know that she has a royal guest." Trembling a little, the skull then addressed the dragon, "Sadly, dragons cannot have questions answered."

"I do not have a question, Mr. Skull, but thank you for letting me know," Seafoam answered him with a nod of her head. The fence intimidated her a little; she didn't know if the humans had noticed the other human skulls that had turned to face their company.

The three of them settled down by the road while they waited. Jack found them a log to sit on while Seafoam curled up nearby and dozed.

While they waited Gabby considered her question. Jack, still in his bodyguard mentality, took stock of the cottage. He could tell that there would be one room– unless the house was more magical than he assumed and was bigger on the inside than it looked on the outside – and that there would not be a lot of things in that cottage. He knew that the skulls were all watching them.

"Baba Yaga," the skull at the gate announced, "you have a visitor."

Moments later the door opened and out stepped somebody approximately her mother's age - the adoptive, not biological - stepped out. "Come in my dear."

The gate opened for Gabby but quickly closed behind her, locking Jack out. "Wait a minute! You cannot go in there alone!" he protested.

Turning around, Gabby smiled before stating, "I'll be okay."

"There is not enough room for three people and a dragon in my cottage," Baba Yaga's voice commanded. "Only the person with the question may enter; that is one of my rules."

"I'll be okay, Jack." Closing her eyes, Gabby added, "I need you to be Ethan right now and trust me."

He watched her enter the cottage. Seconds later he heard the skull next to his hand snapping and removed his hand from the fence. "Sorry."

"It is fine," the skull answered, making a movement that seemed as if it was nodding his head.

The skull next to the gate started speaking, "Our Baba Yaga is not going to eat your princess. The Forest keeps the evil Baba Yaga's from the Princess Questers."

"Unless," another skull added, "it is a Cinderella quester." The skull managed to get a dreamy expression. "Then she gets the difficult tasks Baba Yaga."

"We sense that you do have a question," a skull on the other side of the gate commented. "It is okay to ask."

Jack softened up, dropping his bodyguard stance and once again becoming Ethan. He did have a question to ask but, "I do not want to know the answer. I have been around her for so long, much longer than just our time in this forest. I've had to watch her in the Real World in class and as she spent time with her friends. But I am a Huntsman and Huntsmen do not get involved with the Royal Family."

"They did once," Seafoam piped up, opening a single eye to peer at him. "A long time ago an Alice married a Huntsman. A Cinderella princess married a Huntsman and he became a prince. A Little Mermaid fell in love with a Huntsman instead of her Prince and eloped with him instead of turning into seafoam. Just because the original tales involved Princes does not mean that the Royal Families have to marry Princes now."

A nearby skull, the fourth skull, started talking, "And the original Alice did not start off as a Royal. She was crowned in the second book." Turning to look at the skull next to him, "They also have a long history of not always marrying into other Royal lines."

The skull by the gate piped up again, "Are you certain that you do not want to know the answer to your question?"

"Yes."

Inside the cottage, Gabby observed the carefully made-up bed, the clean floors and empty sink, the closed cabinet doors, and the cat pretending to snooze by the fireplace. When they were situated at the lone table in the cottage Gabby started to speak, "I know I am supposed to bring you something, but I have nothing."

"My dear," Baba Yaga smiled, "the Enchanted Forest has already provided your offering. There was a fresh stack of firewood that appeared at the back of the cottage as soon as my house settled down here. I knew then that the Forest was bringing me a Quester." Handing over a teacup, "How about we chat and you can tell me about your journey before you ask your question? I think your young man needs to decide if he wants to ask his question on not."

"I wish I understood him," she sadly responded.

Giving the Princess in front of her a knowing smile, Baba Yaga gave the girl some grandmotherly advice. "He needs to understand himself first."

"I think I love him," Gabby whispered. "He has been around far more than just our time in the Forest. We have had classes together where I have gotten to hear his opinion about reading assignments. I realize now that he has been following me, but that was part of his job. I've seen him giving classmates meals or helping them pay for food when they were short on cash or used up their meal plan allotments for the week. He let people he didn't even know use some of his copies at the campus computer lab because they had run out of free copies. I have seen him be generous. I have seen him be protective. I have seen him stop fights and prevent them." She paused in the middle of her memories. "Spending all of this undiluted time with him has shown me how he thinks, feels. I don't want to be without him."

Carefully, Baba Yaga pushed this conversation further. "Is your question about him?"

Gabby took a sip as she considered changing her question. "No. Am I going to make a good Queen?"

Baba Yaga's voice deepened as she started to answer the question. "You are going to make a wonderful Queen. Your subjects will adore you and your offspring. Wonderland will experience a prosperous period of time that will be felt in far more than just you and your children's reigns. You will be known as fair and just along with your chosen king by your side."

Gabby smiled as she wrapped Baba Yaga into a hug, "Thank you."

"I wish I could tell you more." She, herself, wondered who the Princess' chosen king would be. However, even Baba Yagas knew that sometimes magic gave a helping hand in forming bonds of True Love.

Looking the old lady in the eyes, Gabby allowed her emotions to show. "That isn't necessary. I know who I would choose to be by my side. He just needs to realize it."

Emerging from the cottage, she watched as Ethan chatted with the skulls and the dragon. It was Baba Yaga who spoke up, "Ethan Jack, do you have a question for me at this time?"

"No, Ma'am."

Giving him a warning, she hoped he would ask just to be able to end the emotional storm brewing between the two. "I cannot guarantee that you will be able to find me again."

Taking a deep breath, Ethan answered her, "I will take that risk. I am not certain if I want my question answered right now or not."

"Understood." All she could do was nod her head in understanding even if she couldn't understand how stubborn a certain Huntsman could be about affairs of the heart.

They left the cottage and as the Baba Yaga waved them off, she asked the skulls about what they talked to Ethan about.

"He loves her but is afraid that he cannot be with her," the gate skull answered.

"I think they will be," another commented.

"I think they won't," the third and fourth added. "He won't do anything because of his perceived responsibilities."

Chapter 8

Closing her eyes, Gabby laid there staring at what stars she could see while thinking instead of sleeping. She was falling in love with Ethan and it scared her.

It was a million little things like the way he had stared at her writing notes in class. The many times he kept her from falling on her face over the logs that the Forest put in her path. He was unlike any of the guys from when she was growing up. None of them would have held her hair back and whispered soothing words while she purged her stomach after the Were-Huntsman debacle.

At night she saw him scratching the top of Sea Foam's head before the wyrmling fell asleep. It was amazing that the little dragon stayed with them after her wings were healed. It was even more amazing how Ethan had taken to her after his initial misgivings.

There were only a few problems, and she suspected they were caused by the Forest's attempts to get Gabby and

Ethan closer together. She needed to be home and the Enchanted Forest was keeping her lost.

Gabby stared at where Ethan…Jack…Ethan…Jack was turning a carefully caught rabbit – they made certain that it was a regular rabbit and not a Talking Rabbit – over a fire. She was thinking and all her thoughts wanted to tangle together into one massive knot.

It was quite obvious that he liked her. Each morning found the pair snuggled closer than before next to the dying embers of the fire. Ethan's arm had her tucked securely into him as his back took on the vulnerable position of being turned towards the forest instead of the fire.

They truly weren't worried; the Were-Huntsman had been Gabby's third and final quest in the Enchanted Forest.

And yet they were no closer to Wonderland than they were to whatever was hidden in the center of the Forest.

It was there. It was waiting. Gabby began to doubt that what the Forest was waiting for was because of her.

When she was honest with herself, she would admit that she'd had a crush on Ethan at school. She had been secretly thrilled the day he had sat next to her in class. She could barely borrow a pencil. She was relieved to see him standing behind her when she realized that she was no longer on her college campus and was in the Enchanted Forest instead.

And now? After spending hours and weeks by his side as she learned about her new home and his life here? As they battled bridges and Were-Huntsman?

She knew she loved him.

She knew it when Howard had locked Ethan in the cellar.

She knew it when she saved them.

She knew it when he carried her out of the cottage and comforted her while she sobbed and retched in the clearing.

That was the thing about fairy tales and she was the product of more than just the Wonderland Tradition. She knew her tales. A merchant's daughter could become a princess. The abused step-sister that ended up going to the ball and meeting a prince. A mermaid that longed to be a human – if you ignored the Grimm tales. A goose girl. A mistreated third son. They could all become a Princess or a Prince if the story demanded it.

Fairy tales were about hope and redemption. They were about warnings and dangers. A quester, or an average person, could gain riches or reptiles all based on how they treated the elderly lady who was really a fairy or a Fairy

Godmother in disguise. Anybody could defeat the hypothetical dragon that threatened their welfare or happiness.

Gabby looked at Ethan…Jack and knew that his side of the tale was the hope side of fairy tales. It was the hope that the youngest son could overcome obstacles and become more than his station in life.

Jack…Ethan…Jack just did not see it.

"Jack?"

"Yes, Princess?" He was frustrated. The fire had refused to start and it was taking him longer than usual for the kindling to catch the tiny flames he was creating.

She took a deep breath before sharing her thoughts. "Every trial is about testing my ability at ascending the throne and ruling a kingdom."

"Yes, Princess." The title was his reminder of who she was in relation to himself.

"The bridge was about analyzing situations and not doing something just because I could especially when there are more important matters that need to be tackled." Even the thoughtful tone in her voice caught his attention.

Jack watched Gabby as she stroked Sea Foam's snout. He imagined that the dragon was warm when everything else around them was cold.

"Sea Foam was about analyzing threats. She wasn't a threat. It also tested my compassion. She was hurt and scared and I helped her instead of jumping to conclusions and killing her."

She stopped to think. "The Granny's Cottage was about finding my way out of tough situations without any help. You were locked in the basement, sorry root cellar, and unable to help. Sea Foam couldn't get into the cottage and if she did anything it would have destroyed everybody in the cottage. It was me against the freakish Wolf-Huntsman hybrid."

"That was scary. What did you call him – a werewolf?"

"It was pure luck that there was a silver knife still in that house."

"It was magic, Gabby. You have to get used to it." He slipped up and forgot to be careful with how he addressed her.

Turning to face him, she grimaced, "You've been calling me 'Princess' all night."

"That is what you are," he stated.

Even though he refused to make eye contact with her, Gabby continued. "Jack…Ethan, you aren't just a Jackson, you are also a Huntsman. We have gone a week without a quest and we are no closer to the castle, any castle, than when we began. If this was my quest, we would have encountered the next trial. I think this one is yours."

"No, Princess," he stood up in protest. He was her bodyguard and he would risk his life to protect her.

She stood there for a moment, not certain what to do. She wanted to stay with Ethan and try to reason with his logic. She could throw out fairy tale after fairy tale in support of her thoughts, but he might counter back with the version of events he had learned.

Acknowledging that she was in a lose-lose situation when it came to him, Gabby stood up and gathered her cloak tightly around her body. "Then I need you to let me continue on this path alone. I cannot keep waiting for you to realize what I figured out at Granny's Cottage. All of the signs were there from the moment I walked into the Never-ending Forest wearing a red cloak with a Huntsman on my heels. If we weren't lying to each other we would admit what was there between us from the moment you sat down next to me in class."

Gabby moved to stand in front of Jack before he could say anything, "You may be called 'Jack' but you really are an Ethan and not Ethan the Extra. You are still the fifth Jack that nobody, including yourself, knows what to do with. You don't even know why you became a Huntsman; you said so yourself."

Taking a deep breath, she said the most difficult part of her thoughts, "So I'm going to ask you to let me go. This isn't just my quest but it's your quest too; you need to find yourself and what you want and need. You need to figure out if you are going to be Jack the Bodyguard or Ethan my friend and consort. Hopefully, you'll find me at the castle when you know."

She left without saying another word. Just left Jack staring at the fire and where Sea Foam was curled up asleep. By noon she was at the Wonderland Bridge.

Chapter 9

Sitting down beneath a giant mushroom, Gabby allowed herself to cry. She had to get it out of her system before getting to the castle gates. She cried for so many things: the family that was left behind, the family she had never met, the mother she would barely get to know, and the loss of Jack…Ethan.

There was one thing Gabby did know and it was that she couldn't think of Jack as anybody but Ethan. Jacks were faceless bodyguards that appeared to live to serve the throne. The Jack/Huntsman combination that had been her companion for the past two weeks was Ethan.

"Why so glum?" a silky voice from above her sighed.

Standing up and away from the mushroom, Gabby noticed the pale purple Caterpillar smoking what looked like a pipe. "Smoking is bad for you."

"So I've been told. Are you going to answer my question?"

"No offense, but no, I'm not. It's personal."

"No offense taken. I assume that you have read the original tale?" the Caterpillar asked.

"Yes, I have. I do know that someday I might come to you or your brothers for cryptic advice when I need to come up with the answer myself but need an impartial sounding board, but what has upset me isn't something that I can fix."

"Wise words from one so young. Time will only tell what is in your clouds. See you again, Princess Gabrielle." With those parting words, the unnamed Caterpillar disappeared in a puff of smoke leaving Gabby coughing.

"I do believe that I'm experiencing my final quest," she whispered, wondering which character would be coming next.

The answer arrived fifteen minutes later in the form of a smiling green Cheshire Cat. "Good morning, my dear," she purred. "I sense you have questions and concerns." The cat floated in circles around Gabby's shocked form.

Smiling, Gabby suddenly had an idea beginning to form in her mind. "The Trickster. You'll twist your words around and manipulate me for your own means."

"Well, I never!" the Cheshire Cat grinned her weirdly pale green grin, her tone indicating the opposite. "My grandfather perhaps…never me," she purred, smiling her sly smile.

"Grandfather?"

"Times ten. It's easier to leave off all of those grands do you not think?"

"Makes sense," Gabby paused. "I'm still not asking you any questions, but I do want to make a deal with you." The idea she had in mind was beginning to make workable sense.

Floating around Gabby once more, "Deals are tricky businesses."

"I know."

"Are you certain you want to do this?" She was floating around upside down now.

Gabby paused, noting the Cheshire's hesitance, "Would you rather I tell you my plan first?"

The Cheshire Cat thought for a moment, gradually disappearing starting from her tail. Half of her body was gone before she reformed. "What is the deal?"

"You seem to be a good judge of character; you should be able to tell if somebody means harm or good. If anybody asks you for directions you simply…misdirect them however you deem fit and then warn me or my Cards."

The Cheshire started fading out again. "Anyway, I see fit?"

"Get them lost, send them on a never-ending path that leads back to the Never-ending Forest, or direct them to an obstacle course. Whatever indirect means you can think of that won't kill them."

"Maim?"

"No violence. Maybe scare them a bit."

"What if violence is their goal?"

"Then violent and scary is a fit punishment for wanting to hurt a relatively peaceful land."

Cheshire solidified for a moment. "You met the Were-Huntsman," she purred.

"Yes, I did." Gabby saw no reason to lie about the experience. She had a feeling that it was now common knowledge around the lands.

"He was the only one of his kind, so far."

"Thank you. If Ethan…I mean Jack Huntsman runs into you and hasn't searched his soul yet, please direct him on a journey that will." Gabby avoided looking at Cheshire, afraid of what expression the Cat was wearing.

"Yes, Princess," she, as always, purred, but this time there was a note of interest in the sound.

The Cheshire then vanished, content with her role of being allowed to wreck mischief for the Princess. Gabby watched, amazed, as she disappeared from both ends.

Chapter 10

Fifteen minutes later, she was still walking, looking around every corner expecting another Wonderland character or experience. Where was the backward checkerboard? Tweedle Dum or Dee? The Mad Hatter? The road was becoming less of a dirt path and more of a smooth pebble road. She could see a small town about a half-mile away.

It was a strange little town, from what she could see. Bright reds and purples stood out. Coming closer she noticed that the reds and purples were all at one building that was shaped like a teapot. Everything around it was muted blues, greens, grays, and brick in various natural brick shades.

"Hatter's Tea Shoppe" read the sign over the door. "Wonderland's Best Selection of Teas and Hats" read the smaller words on the window and door.

"What an odd combination," Gabby commented mostly to herself until she realized that the tea-drinking Mad Hatter owned the shop with the March Hare and Dormouse.

Gabby faced a dilemma. She could enter the shop and meet these apparently colorful characters or continue on to the castle. Each idea had its merits, and she knew that it was a trial. Now that she knew what was being tested, she could figure out when it was happening.

She just couldn't figure out what the right answer was when meeting the Mad Hatter could also mean delaying her coronation. Which was more important?

With a sigh, Gabby followed her instincts when she pushed open the door and entered the store that looked like a rainbow had puked in it. Brightly colored hats with insects, flowers, and ribbons lined the walls. Shelves and shelves of tea boxes took up space along the floor, littered by tea test centers. One corner even had a build-you-own-hat station with a build-your-own-tea station in the opposite corner. Three cash drawers were located near the door.

The biggest spectacles were on the floor. The Mad Hatter was center stage at his podium calling out sales to customers, or calling the March Hare back to his side. While the Dormouse slept in his teapot and the Hatter pushed sales, the March Hare would manically hop around the store, interrupting employees, and creating confusion.

It took the March Hare running into Gabby for the not-quite Mad Hatter to notice that the March Hare was running amuck.

"Hare!" Hatter snapped, adjusting his hat as he approached the pair. "How much Happy Hare Energy Tea did you drink from the demo stations?"

"Um…" the Hare hopped in place. Holding up four fingers, "Three? Maybe?"

Speaking into a small microphone on his lapel, "Genie, please bring some calming tea to Hare," was announced over the speakers.

Turning to Gabby, "It puts him out like a light." Holding out a hand, "Madeline Hatter, pleased to meet you. You can call me Liny."

"Ummm, Gabby," she responded, slightly confused.

"I know. We've been expecting you."

"I thought that you were a 'he'," Gabby stammered out past her shock.

"It's a wig. I'm naturally a blond," she whispered, tugging at the crazy orange hair topped with a purple top hat.

"I don't want people to completely know my true identity. They think that I'm my long-lost brother Madder."

"Where is Madder?"

"He became too mad to run the shop so we sent him to Old Mother Hubbard's Shoe for Behavioral and Cognitive Adjustments." Hatter started walking around straightening hats and tea boxes.

Following behind Hatter, Gabby asked, "In the Never-ending Forest?"

"Right next to Sleeping Beauty's land."

"Duly noted."

"March Hare has been twice and I'll be talking to his sister about sending him again. He doesn't like to take his meds." They watched as a passed-out Hare was carried away by the Tweedles. They both waved at the Princess before disappearing into a rabbit hole hidden by a hat display.

"I'm glad you stopped in," Hatter whispered. "I wish I could stay and chat, but business is business. I'll be by the castle later to drop off the Queen's tea order. You might want to look around if you want your own tea order, but not today. The castle is waiting."

"Thank you. I've learned so much from you these past ten minutes."

"Stop by any time on Tuesdays." Hatter straightened a hat that had tilted sideways. "It's my slowest day." Looking around, "Now, please excuse me, I have to go back to pretending to be my manic-depressive brother."

Gabby's head jerked at the slightly outdated psychological terminology. "Huh," she mumbled. "Madder Hatter is bipolar, interesting." With one last look around the Tea Shoppe, she took in the organization beneath the chaos and hoped that Madeline would continue to be the head operating manager at the store. Gabby could only imagine how things would fall apart by having an unmediated manic not keeping the shop in order.

Looking at the road ahead of her, she faced the path that would lead to the castle. She figured out that the Tea Shoppe was to show her that well-balanced management would make for a well-run kingdom even if the outer layer is an illusion of madness and chaos.

Chapter 11

Weeks after her twenty-first birthday, Gabby finally found herself on the steps of the Wonderland Castle. She imaged the leaves in her hair and wondered why everybody reacted to her as if she was clean and not covered in a thick layer of dirt.

"I'm not ready for this," she whispered to herself.

The guards at the door weren't aware of that fact when the one on the left responded with, "It will be fine. They have been waiting for you easily for nineteen years."

The cadence of his speech patterns calmed her down, reminding her of Ethan. "I'm a mess. I'm covered in dirt and leaves."

"Nobody notices," the guard to her right answered. "As soon as you crossed the Wonderland Bridge Wonderland put a glamour on your appearance. Only a few gifted people can see you as you currently are."

"What am I wearing?"

The guard on the left responded, "A blue dress. Alice in Wonderland colors. Your hair is down and clean." Turning back to his post, "Go on inside, Your Highness."

"Is my mother well?"

"Perfectly healthy."

"I was told she was dying."

"Jack was told to tell you that. Do not blame him. He only knew the lie."

"Thank you."

Placing her hand on the door, she knew that one push would be all that it took to change her from Gabby to Gabrielle. She never really thought about the power of names until she saw two different sides to her bodyguard. For a moment she wondered how he would act when he was being "Extra" instead of the friendly Ethan or the steadfast and protective Jack. Maybe he would feel insecure and unneeded.

Suddenly, she turned around, "You're one of Jack's brothers, aren't you?"

Bowing slightly, "Yes ma'am. I'm your Spade and a little surprised that Jack isn't with you."

"I had to leave him behind," she paused. "He needed to do some soul searching." All Gabby knew was that he would never be Extra to her. She just wondered how Ethan Jack would fit into Gabrielle's life.

Pushing those thoughts away, she entered the life she never knew existed.

    Waiting in front of their thrones, The King and Queen of Wonderland each remembered their first impressions of the Castle.

    The Queen remembered the hanging banners that spanned the entrance with the most clarity. On one side hung the banners for the Hearts and the Clubs. On the other side hung the banners for the Spades and the Diamonds. In the center of the quartz floor was a huge twenty by twenty-foot design with the suits in their own quadrants. Even today she would enter the hall to remind herself of the fragile unity that Wonderland had forged before they could become one kingdom.

One kingdom brought together by one girl. It was a weighty responsibility that was passed down through the generations. A weighty responsibility that was started by somebody accidentally discovering just the right portal into Wonderland.

The King remembered the sparkle of black, silver, and red flecks of a glittering quartz floor in the light of thousands of candles. Even today he could barely resist the urge to touch the red-veined white granite columns that flanked the doors and framed the banners.

The ballroom had been slightly better with black, red, and gold flecks in the stone. Those columned were black-veined, but the then Princess Alice the Fifth had caught his attention and heart; a tugging from his heartstrings had directed him to where she had been holding court with her would-be suitors.

Years later and they were still linked by their hearts.

Gareth was not so lucky to be able to wonder about Gabby's impressions on the castle-like his parents were and was quietly considering the eventual meeting with his baby sister. He had grown up among those columns that fascinated his father. He had hidden behind those banners that left his mother breathless in awe. The pomp and circumstance of the castle never were given the opportunity to impress him. He had no reason to think about Gabby's impressions of the very place he had grown up in; he wondered if she could remember the teddy bear he had given her before she had to leave Wonderland. He wondered if she would get along with his wife, Mary.

Chapter 12

Ethan stumbled over logs and into holes, cursing the forest and the disappearing road.

Sea Foam the dragon had already given up and taken to the skies. On occasion he could look up and catch a glimpse of the little dragon, using her as a beacon to guide his way home.

It had been a week. He was going to miss the assignment of Gabby's additional guards. He secretly hoped to be one of the Huntsmen selected to protect her. If he could not be with her, then he definitely wanted to be in a position where he could watch out for her, even if watching her marry and have children with somebody else would break his heart. It was better than being the Card that would be her primary bodyguard. Ethan wondered which brother would have that honor.

With a plop into a pile of wet leaves, Ethan sighed. He already missed her laugh. He had fallen for it ever since that first day in Dr. Beyer's literature class. It had been pure chance that he had sat down next to her in class; he had no clue about what she would look like, only that she would be in that class. The only class he had planned on taking.

If he did not get up and start moving, he would lose sight of Sea Foam and would be lost in the middle of the Enchanted Forest. He was not even certain if he had crossed over into Wonderland Territory even though he did not see any bridges. A bridge really meant very little; they had been known to disguise themselves into more and less elaborate crossings.

He would give anything to see a talking flower. At least almost anything. Not his heart; he had already given that way.

Looking up, could he really stand around guarding her while she was happy with somebody else? Did he really want to give up his chance to be with her and…where was Sea Foam?

The forest was moving him around in circles. He could not count how many times he had seen that tree stump or this track that Sea Foam had left behind. Plopping down on a tree stump, Jack looked up into the sky and wondered what he was doing wrong.

Sea Foam landed without stirring up any dust and curled herself up to stare at Jack. "Are you Ethan right now or Jack?"

"I never understood that," Jack admitted. "She kept switching back and forth between the two."

"That's because," the little dragon began to explain, "sometimes you were friendly and nice and then you were Ethan. Other times, when you were being Jack, you were stern and unyielding. You were all business and no fun." Letting out a snort that ruffled some leaves around them, Sea Foam looked at him blankly. "Ethan pulled Princess closer and Jack pushed her away."

"So, who am I being right now?"

Tilting her head, "Are you missing Princess or do you want to get back to being a Huntsman."

"I miss Gabby," he sighed, leaning against the tree that was behind his make-shift seat. "I shouldn't have pushed her away."

Suddenly a bridge appeared within his line of vision. The supports looked like mushrooms and various gemstones and colored stones sparkled in the sun. Sea Foam's eyes widened when she noticed that they were shaped like the card suits.

"Wow!" she breathed. "So pretty."

Suddenly a voice echoed around them, calling for the small dragonet. "Sea Foam!"

"Mam!" the turquoise dragon perked up. "That's my mother. I wish you luck and when you see Princess again let her know that I'll visit someday." Without another word she leaped into the air and flew away, leaving Jack alone with his thoughts.

Taking a deep breath, he stood and went to cross over the Wonderland Bridge.

He had not made it very many paces on the other side of the bridge when he heard a purring sound. Lounging in some branches over Jack's head, he noticed a green Cheshire

Cat. "I see you have finally realized what our dear Princess already knew."

"Yes, I love her and want to be with her."

"Good," and with a wave of her paw, the brown leaves transformed into the talking flowers, who were upset because he nearly sat on some of them. The road reformed underneath Ethan's feet, showing him the way home. To Gabby.

Chapter 13

Standing before the gates, Jack was not aware that the message he should have been learning had not completely sunk in. The journey through the forest was not just for Gabby but for himself also. Through those woods, he recognized, the princess learned how to think on her feet and use whatever knowledge she had gained in her previous life towards making wise decisions as a monarch. Not everything was as it appeared, especially in Wonderland, and it was important that she recognize those lessons.

But Jack could not quite grasp what his lesson was supposed to be. He loved Gabby with all of his heart, but could not see how he was important towards the kingdom. He was a Card. He was a Huntsman. He was Jack. Not Ethan. Not Ethan Jack. He was Jack.

"Hello, Brother," one of the guards greeted him. "I met the princess days ago."

"Hello, Spade," the Huntsman bowed.

"No, I'm not the Spade right now, I'm your brother," Stephan interrupted. "We are more than just our jobs, you know."

"No, I don't know," Jack answered his brother. Staring up at the castle in front of him, he started thinking. "Why did I have to be the Princess' tracker?"

Shaking his head, Stephan stated something that caught Jack off guard, "Did you know that our father was the Queen's tracker? That's why Father was the Head Card instead of a Heart."

Tilting his head, Jack turned to look at his brother, "Why wasn't somebody else the Queen's tracker?"

"Because Father was the right age and Uncle was too young at the time. He is a year younger than the Queen…"

The townspeople always wondered about the relationship between the Queen and her retired Spade. Even today their father held the Queen's ear whenever important matters were happening. They were the best of friends.

"What does that have to do with anything?"

"The Royal Family of Wonderland always has a connection with their Cards," Stephan stated matter-a-fact. "It's that Tracker Bond that nobody really talks about." Straightening up as people started approaching the gates,

Stephan transformed into the Spade right in front of Jack's eyes.

Greeting the people who were approaching, the Spade was all business with his tone. "Welcome to the Palace. State your name and business."

The man straightened up and cleared his throat before announcing, "I'm Brayson Riverstone and I am one of the tutors for the Princess."

"Which tutor?" the Spade questioned while scanning the admittance lists.

"Protocol."

"And you?"

"Mary Edmunds. Manners."

The Princess already has impeccable manners, Jack thought bitterly while looking at the prudish looking woman covered head to toe in shades of blue that masked her figure.

"Dancy Price. Dancing Master." He bowed as he introduced himself before his nose went into the air...

Jack watched carefully as his brother scanned for each name on the list. He wondered how bored Gabby would be learning about Wonderland History. He wondered if these tutors knew about the Wonderland Underground and the Wonderland Aboveground. He wondered if they could tell her about the Enchanted Forest and its unrecorded legends. He wondered so many things but did not voice them out loud.

After five minutes of checking names against faces and IDs, the Spade finally allowed the small army of tutors to enter through the gates. Within moments he was back to being Stephan, Ethan's brother, but Ethan was still Jack the Huntsman. "We aren't robots," Stephan whispered. "We are allowed to feel and love and every other emotion in between."

How could he know that Jack was not listening? Back to his protocols, Jack grabbed a piece of paper from the Guards' Stand and started writing a note. It was not a long note, but it was long enough to break the Princess's heart.

Princess,

I'm sorry. I can't love you.

Jack

Part Two

Chapter 19

Two Years Later

There was one thing that Gabby wasn't used to and that was dresses. A tomboy at heart, she had to adjust to the standards between the world where she was raised and the world where her biological family lived. It was maddening.

She was now completely accepted as a member of the royal family and all the necessary training was frustrating. Things like which fork or spoon to use, how to walk down the stairs gracefully, how to sit down without wrinkling her skirts were all things that she never dreamed she would actually use before Wonderland.

That was how she divided her lives: Before Wonderland and After Wonderland. Before Ethan and After Ethan.

Before.

After.

Before her heart was rejected and after her heart was smashed into a million teeny, tiny pieces.

Smashed. Stomped on. Ground into the tile with the heel of his hiking boots. Rejected by the first person she could see a future with…

Even two years later her parents would look at each other with worried expressions painted on their faces after watching her wander around the castle aimlessly with a book in her hands.

That was just one of the many lies Ethan had told her before he was no longer Ethan her friend and became Jack the Huntsman that she never had to see because he was sent on a mission to hunt out more were-huntsmen. He was sent out even though the Cheshire Cat has assured them that Howard had been the only one of his kind.

No, her mother never had been sick. The urgency was because Gabby would be spending the four years between her 21st and 25th birthdays training to take over the throne. It was Tradition.

It was a Tradition that she would be getting rid of as soon as she had her first daughter.

But first, she had to find her Prince Charming.

That was a bit difficult to do when Ethan stubbornly still owned her heart.

Lesson after lesson moved by with an agonizing degree of slowness.

Posture meant walking with a book on her head – a book she would rather be reading. At first, it was only walking up and down hallways until she started walking while reading from another book – usually for another lesson. Then it was walking up and down the stairs over and over again. Once that was mastered, they had her dancing with a book on her head.

Some days she would stare out the window, watching the Cards and soldiers practicing their swordplay. Whenever she asked about when she would be learning about fencing her parents and tutors would hem and haw before redirecting her towards another lesson that was "absolutely essential."

Dresses and even more dresses meant fittings and standing still for hours upon hours. Gabby would be afraid to move in fear of being stabbed by a pin.

"Why do I need so many dresses?" she would ask. Day dresses. Dining dresses. Morning dresses. Ball gowns. Royal function dresses.

Too much time standing around thinking. Missing Ethan Jack. Wondering what he was doing. Mentally slapping herself for missing him and wondering why she couldn't get him out of her heart or her head.

History lessons were no better. The Princess was fully instructed in the history of Wonderland including the parts not chronicled. Traditions and legends that even the tutors and Cards were unaware of.

"Are you serious?" she asked, looking at the crest above the throne. The information her…Mother the Queen had just shared surprised the Princess. "But the books…"

"Haven't you learned by now that the published story isn't always the real tale?"

Staring at her biological mother sitting on the throne – not yet capable of calling this stranger "Mother" or anything other than 'Your Majesty' – Gabby made a huge decision. She would not foster out any of her future children.

"I'm not graceful!" The shout echoed throughout the ballroom where the Princess was practicing her dance steps. "Of course, I'm going to step on your feet!"

The Dancing Instructor – as she mentally called him – ahem, Dancing Master huffed. "You can walk down the stairs with a book on your head."

"Just because I can put two feet in front of each other doesn't mean I can follow this complicated 'pattern' of dance steps you are trying to jam into my over-packed brain. Of course, I'm going to step on your feet! This dance has no pattern to learn!" Jerking the heels off of her feet, Gabby tossed one in the direction of her Card.

Stephan ducked, moving quickly enough to miss the shoe as it hit the wall behind him. Shaking his head, he left his position and joined the frustrated duo.

"Mirror me," he instructed her, ignoring the sputtering coming from the Dancing Master's mouth.

Gabby watched the Spade move through the first set of steps before mimicking his moves. After a few tries, she had gotten it down.

Stephan then added three more steps to the pattern. The entire process took hours – hours she gladly missed with her etiquette tutors – but in the end, Gabby had mastered the Wonderland Waltz.

It had taken the Dancing Master weeks to get her to that point and it took Stephan five hours to help the Princess master the dance.

"Seriously!" the master huffed. "It took a mere Card to teach you this dance! Blood will tell."

The dancers froze at his insult. The Spade took a step backward when he noticed the audience in the background.

It would have done the dancing master a lot of good to have noticed that the Spade was slipping from Stephan and back into a bodyguard. His rant continued, insulting the Princess in every capacity that he could think of.

"Just whose blood are you insulting?" the King's voice boomed as he fully entered the room after allowing the tutor's spiel to fade away.

Simpering, the tutor bowed, "Not you, Your Highness."

"My wife's blood then?" the King pretended to ask.

"No, Your Majesty."

"Then how does my daughter's blood 'tell' anything other than her birth and fostering?"

Whispering, fear infusing his voice, the master answered, "She spent weeks in the Enchanted Forest with a Huntsman, Sire." Standing a bit taller as he began to feel ever more confident, he continued, "Everybody has seen her pining for Jack Huntsman for over a year now and it is embarrassing to the Crown."

The Spade straightened even more. He knew that Ethan Jack ending what was forming between the pair hadn't been an easy decision. He had done what he had deemed best for the Crown and Wonderland, even if he still suffered for his decision. He even tried to unsuccessfully replace Princess Gabrielle from his heart.

Then again, Stephan reflected, Ethan would be a Spade and it would never be easy for a Spade to move on from their soulmate. He knew this from personal experience.

"Do you need my assistance removing," the Spade sneered in the dancing master's direction, "him from the Castle, Your Majesty?"

"No," the King answered. "Diamond!"

"Yes, Your Highness?" Derek appeared from nowhere. He covertly winked at his brother.

"Escort the dancing," he paused, "instructor to the gates. Make certain that his name is removed from the list."

The demoted master's eyes widened. "Your Highness," he pleaded.

"A Master does not insult his charge. He learns and discovers how the charge learns and adjusts his methods. The Princess has been telling you for weeks that she cannot process the steps and it took her bodyguard to teach her. You then insulted her, her parentage, the Huntsmen Organization, and the Card family. These walls have ears and you'll be lucky if you get another job in Wonderland again all because you gave voice to your arrogance."

The King remained standing proudly as the Diamond led the tutor from the room. The Princess stood in awe as the King watched the whining tutor resisting the Diamond's attempts at getting him to leave the room.

"Why?"

"I'd heard your complaints but couldn't do anything about them until today," he explained. Shaking his head, "And I was able to do something fatherly towards you for once."

"Thank you." She surprised the King by giving him a hug.

"Now, show me what the Spade taught you."

Smiling, the Princess curtsied before her father before the pair danced across the floor.

Staring at the forks and spoons lined up in front of her, Princess Gabrielle was more than tempted to take one of the forks and start combing her hair with it. She knew that nobody would get the reference, but it would be worth it simply to annoy Madam Edmunds and Master Riverstone.

She knew many things, including that the Widow Edmunds was having a love affair with the stuffy Riverstone. The Princess already knew which fork to use for what course; it had been one of the many seemingly pointless lessons that the Harrington's had her learn.

That didn't mean that her etiquette tutors didn't constantly quiz her on the usage of silverware. It made

Gabby want to pick her teeth using a dessert spoon as a mirror even more tempting.

Now, lessons on pouring tea during tea time would be valuable, but her request fell on deaf ears and Master Riverstone 'knew what was best.'

"What is wrong with this place setting?" Master Riverstone's monotone asked the daydreaming princess.

"Nothing, "Gabby answered. "I…"

"Of course, something is wrong," he interrupted her.

"I already fixed the mix-up with the fish and salad forks," Gabrielle stated, standing up from her place, setting her folded napkin on her plate. "I switched the wine and water glasses when you were looking at yourself in the mirror. The napkin was in the wrong place, but since I was sitting down its proper placement became my lap."

Princess Gabrielle started to leave before turning around. "If you were more observant you would have seen that I had already mastered dining room etiquette and have ever since I was thirteen years old. Just because I have not always lived here doesn't mean I am clueless."

She reached the door when she added, "Tomorrow I expect lessons about Tea Time and serving tea because that was something I didn't have an opportunity to learn. If you cannot fulfill this request, I will insist on finding new tutors."

Gliding through the doorway, the Princess refused to excuse herself. It was a haughty yet royal privilege that she could enjoy using when the situation called for it.

"Brava," the Spade pretended to applaud her. "About time, Your Majesty."

Shaking her head, "They both know it is the end of their careers and school if they are fired by the royal family."

"And the maids will talk."

"And listen at peepholes," Gabby added.

"Oh no, Your Royalness," the Spade grinned. "That's the fives and sixes."

"Of course," she sighed. "I never asked why you and your brothers promoted the tens to bodyguard status."

The Spade went still before answering her carefully. "Added precautions. There have been rumblings about an uprising ever since your return."

"Where are the other bodyguards?"

"They aren't supposed to be seen, Princess."

"I see," she answered even though she did not.

Chapter 15

One Year Later

Watching their daughter stare out of the window instead of at the book she was supposed to be studying, Queen Alice the Fifth turned to look at her husband, Traylor Erickson, with distress in her eyes. This should be a happy time for Gabrielle.

"What should we do?"

"We cannot do anything," he reminded her. "But we can make that idiot Huntsman jealous."

"Ethan Jack is not an idiot."

"He broke our daughter's heart; he is not good enough for her."

Patting him on the hand, "Nobody will ever be good enough for your little girl."

"True."

"But we live in a land of fairy tales and the fantastic and there are the Traditions that must be followed."

Traylor looked over at his wife and sighed. He hated balls. All of that dancing and standing around talking to people you truly disliked gave him a headache. It was a good thing that it would take a while for his wife to plan it. A good long while. These types of things had to be planned and timed carefully.

Impatiently tapping her toes under the table, Princess Gabrielle watched and listened while the King added a new lesson to her schedule: chess.

She wanted to ask why.

Why chess?

What importance was a board game when she was still incapable of using a diplomatic tongue?

"Bishops are the only pieces that can move diagonally," the King instructed her while demonstrating on the black and white board.

Finally, impatience overtook Gabby's tongue. "Why is this important?"

"Don't you remember the chess game in *Through the Looking Glass*?"

"Yes, everything moved backward."

"Everything moved in reverse of what Alice expected," he corrected. "At the end of the game, once she figured out what she was doing, Alice was crowned. It's how we were able to take over the throne."

From somewhere inside her Gabby knew and added, "Wonderland helped."

"Wonderland was tired of destructive chaos and madness."

"Right. Controlled chaos and madness are much better." She started to think about how Liny Hatter kept her shop with the appearance of chaos, but she had actually organized that madness into a show.

"Actually, yes," the King smiled.

Setting the game pieces back into position, the King gestured for her to start the game. "Remember to protect your king. While the queen has the biggest range of motion, it is all lost without the king."

"But…" Gabby started thinking. In Wonderland the Queen was the most important position, but she also knew that her mother would be lost without her father.

"Yes," he sighed, "if something happened to your mother you would be the Queen and I'd be demoted, but Wonderland is not stable without both its King and Queen. Choose wisely. Not all Queens have found their True Love."

"And if it's Ethan Jack?" she worriedly asked.

"Then you'll just have to play a long game."

The King wasn't paying attention to the game as they were playing until Gabby whispered, "Checkmate."

Looking at the game board, the King stammered, "How?"

"Preston Harrington taught me. I guess he thought it would be useful to understand game strategy." Catching the King's crestfallen expression, she added, "But I never really understood all of that information about the king and queen."

Still staring at the board, he asked, "Just how good are you?"

"It got to the point where we'd play the pieces on the opposite side of the board from us."

He examined the board, "Why?"

"Because Alice had to play the game backward and that was one of my favorite stories growing up," Gabby explained as she set the board up. "I was eleven and wanted to try it. It took three years to beat my… Preston."

The room-filling with tension thick enough to cut, they looked anywhere but at each other. It was a reminder that the Princess had more than one set of parents.

She wondered if she would ever see them again.

Chapter 16

One Year Later

It never made much sense about why the Royal family had to travel by carriage in order to get to Neverland. There was magic everywhere! Why couldn't a portal be created?

Several people stiffened when Gabby shared her thoughts.

"It's too risky," the King finally answered her.

The Neverland Festival of Lights was supposed to be a unifying event that would bring all the Neverland Kingdoms together for one week. It occurred every twenty-five years.

It would be the first time that Mary and Gareth would make a major public appearance in front of the Five Neverland Kingdoms.

The Wonderland royals were invited because of Gareth. The council decided it would be rude to exclude his family even though they weren't born in Neverland.

This year the event would be held near Mermaid Lagoon. The Pirates would be docked just outside the mermaid's territory and supposedly they had a massive firework display planned.

The Piccaninny Tribe – they refused to refer to themselves as a kingdom – led by a descendant of the never forgotten Tiger Lily – had camped out near the bluffs, their campfires catching the Neverland residents' attention.

The fairies darted around the campgrounds, playing tricks and creating mild havoc. Sometimes one of them would help another person with something like fixing a pot or lighting a fire.

The others, the Neverland humans from the towns and trees, had scattered themselves among the campgrounds.

Holding her finger to her lips, Mary pushed a knot on a tree and secreted the Royal Family into a hidden tunnel.

The Lost Boys observed Princess Gabrielle as she examined at the space around her. She was amazed that so much space could be carved out from underneath the already massive tree above them.

"How is this possible?" she breathed. While it would have taken her family and the Jacks to circle the tree, this space was easily double, if not more, the diameter of the tree.

The tow-headed boy holding her bag answered her. "Magic." Picking up the bag that was almost as big as he was, he continued. "Both Neverland and fairy magic."

"What is your name?" she asked him.

"Bird," he answered her. "I'm very good at bird calls." Pointing at a little girl. "That's my sister, Robyn."

"I thought the Lost Boys were all boys."

Leading her towards her room, Bird laughed. "Robyn isn't a Lost Boy. She runs errands for Cook." Pulling the heavy bag just a tiny way, he added, "The Lost Boys are like your Deck of Cards. The older ones are bodyguards for the Royal family and the younger ones, like me, run errands and train. Someday I'm going to be one of the patrols."

The little boy puffed up and stood straighter as he showed the Princess her room. He reminded her of past friends' younger siblings who tried to act older than they actually were in hopes of impressing their older sisters' friends.

"If you need anything just pull that cord. Either I or Robyn will appear." With those final words, he disappeared.

"That was one talkative young man," the Spade stated from the doorway.

"Can you blame him? Tending a Royal from another kingdom might feel like an honor for him." Lifting her bag off the floor, she moved it to the bed to begin unpacking.

Quietly he responded, "I suppose so," before disappearing into his own room next door. There was a secret passage that connected the two rooms.

"Do you think Henry and Charlie are enjoying bunking together?" she called after him.

"Of course not. Jacks aren't known for sharing and both of them are already missing their families."

"What about you? You've never mentioned your own family."

Stephan turned around before answering her. "Spades are... different. We take a long time to recover after heartbreak. It's the curse of being an upside-down heart. Henry will have the same problem. We feel more, but

Hearts wear their emotions on their sleeves and Spades bottle it up."

Gabby tilted her head while she considered his words. "Like your heart had a stopper if you flipped a spade upside down."

"Exactly." Taking a dress from her hands, he moved to the hanging roots that served as a closet. "Years ago, before you arrived here, I fell in love. She was amazing, but her father didn't want her marrying a Card. He claimed that my job was too dangerous, even though I wasn't guarding you yet. I was overseeing training and taking shifts at the Palace Gates. On occasion, I would be sent off to check on a rumor and confirm its validity."

He took another dress from her hands.

"What happened to her?"

"They moved. He married her off to a farmer who died in an accident two years ago."

"If you could get her back, would you?"

"In a heartbeat," Stephan looked at the Princess. "Ethan is the same way."

"Right," she snorted.

"Princess," Stephan stated. "Trust me and the powers that be."

"I'll pray you are right."

Watching people zip line through the trees, the Princesses both wished they could join in. Mary quietly held a hand to her stomach and Gabby wished for her jeans.

"Were those the weird blue pants you wore when you returned to Wonderland?" the Queen asked her daughter.

"Yes."

Chuckling, "They wouldn't fit even if you still had them," she stated.

"What do you mean?"

"The maids were complaining about the two inches you grew and the ten pounds you have gained since you have been here."

"What?"

"That's what Wonderland does, my dear. I gained twenty-five pounds before I leveled out. And it's all muscle too. Your activity levels have changed."

Sighing, Gabby looked over to where the Jacks were goofing off with the Lost Boys. A hand fidgeting with her skirts hinted at what she was thinking.

Grabbing her hand, Mary pulled Gabby up. "Come on. I have exactly what you need."

A pair of brown leggings was the first thing Mary handed over to the bewildered Gabby. "Long skirts aren't always practical here, but going bare-legged is a no-go."

Next was a considerably shorter and less full skirt that fell to Gabby's knees. A bodice was layered over that, hiding the closure to the skirt.

Finally, was a pair of knee-high lace-up boots. "They originally had buttons, but that takes forever to put on and off. One of our explorers brought back some boots like these and a pair with zippers, but we can't reproduce the zippers yet."

Standing up, Gabby looked at herself in the mirror. A green and brown vision stood in front of her. She had never worn something quite like this and it had her thinking of a woodcutter's daughter.

"Princess," came from the other side of the door.

"Yes!" they both answered.

"Sorry. Princess Gabrielle, are you ready?" the Spade asked.

Leaning in towards her, Mary whispered, "How are you not in a relationship with him?"

"He's my bodyguard and Ethan's brother."

"It's been over four years."

Smiling weakly, Gabby looked at her sister-in-law before carefully answering her unspoken question, "I know. I can't explain it. I wish I could move on, but it's like something won't let me."

She wasn't aware that he was watching her. Ethan Jack had almost turned down his brothers' invitations to join them. On one hand, the Neverland Festival of Lights only happened every twenty-five years and it was by invitation only for non-Neverlandians. On the other hand, he would constantly be on the lookout for the Princess.

Stephan constantly told him to stop fighting it. They had no control over what was in their deck of cards.

He was speechless when he saw her in everyday Neverland attire. It wasn't often that she wore muted colors like the greens and browns in the outfit she wore.

Sneaking up behind Ethan, Henry began to speak. "I don't know why you are fighting it."

"I am a Card and a Huntsman and she's a princess."

"Wonderland doesn't care." Shaking his head, "Do you want to start moping around like Stephan?" Henry asked.

"No."

"Well, that's where you are heading. She's a breath of fresh air and Wonderland is already flourishing under her appearance."

"To the demise of formal speech," Ethan grumbled.

"Oh, quit being so stuffy, Ethan, as my daughter would say." Henry turned to leave his brother. "Don't carry around the biggest regret of your life."

The Heart left him to watch as Gabby finally took her turn on the zip line. Her shouts of laughter filled the trees and his heart.

It was beginning to make sense why Mary never brought any clothes with her whenever she came to visit. Wonderland and Neverland's styles were vastly different. Mary would have received so many disapproving looks if she came to Wonderland wearing the shorter skirts that were custom here.

"Now, Gabby," she whispered as she pulled out another shorter skirt, "you know these are shorter than you are used to…"

"I've seen shorter," Gabby interrupted, thinking about the miniskirts that her friends had favored, or the pencil skirts her… Michaela wore to work.

"Seriously?" Mary asked, looking at the knee-length skirts. "Shorter?"

Gabby demonstrated with her hands, holding back her laughter as Mary's eyes widened dramatically.

Shaking her head, "Dancing is different too," Mary added. "You'd trip over your skirts in that dress."

"Fine," Gabby sighed. She dismissed the long skirt that had become a security blanket. Reaching into Mary's closet, she pulled out a skirt that made her think of Ethan's eyes when they appeared more green than brown.

Shaking her head, Mary pried the skirt from Gabby's hands and handed over a blue skirt and bodice. "I can't completely go against your mother's wishes. I still have to live with her as my mother-in-law."

"She could live for years."

"Decades."

"That would be nice," Gabby whispered. "I'm not ready to take over the throne yet." Even she knew that her twenty-fifth birthday and coronation were quickly approaching.

"I'm certain you'll have many more years to get to know your parents."

Taking the blue dress, she turned to let her maid help her get into the complicated bodice. Laces – white ribbon – crisscrossed in the back.

"I know I'm lacing this wrong," Stella stated, "but the bow at the back of your spine and trailing down your skirt would be so pretty."

"Just make sure you securely knot it. I'll end up untying it if you don't."

"Wait!" Mary protested, holding up a length of dark blue sash.

The Spade cleared his throat from where he was facing the wall. "Excuse me, but Princess Gabrielle is a young woman in her twenties, not a young girl. I think she would look more mature without any bows. Change the lacings to dark blue. Use the sash to make a belt that is tied on her left side in the front."

"How does he know this stuff?"

"He has a sister," Gabby answered before he could respond. "Jill is younger than Ethan."

Mary remained silent as she considered the Spade's words. "There's a braid-style I'd like to try before we put your hair in a low knot," she suggested, touching the base of her neck. "The mermaids call it a fishtail braid."

Hidden among the crowd, Ethan watched Princess Gabrielle descend the stairs into the ballroom. Nobody expected her to be able to perform the Neverlandian dance steps, but he glowered as she attempted them with various heads of state.

It was so tempting.

"Mother cursed you with your name," Stephan sighed when he caught up with Ethan. "It's the curse of the Spade to always love someone but have to keep it stoppered up."

"How do you know?" Ethan asked his older brother, looking somewhere other than Gabby for the first time in hours.

"I can feel you tracking her across the ballroom. Unless you are going to ask her to dance, I need you to stop. I can't block you and the other people watching her in order to track the threats."

"Is she being threatened?" Jack jerked to attention.

Stephan snorted as he felt the change from Jack to Huntsman take over his brother's body. "I always wondered how that worked. Your transformation from Jack to Huntsman."

"The Princess calls me Ethan or Jack whenever I was one or the other. I couldn't explain that I couldn't control my instincts."

His brother looked at him, "And they are becoming less formal. Changes are coming."

"What do you mean?"

"I can't tell you."

"You certainly can."

"Stay in Huntsman mode a bit longer. You'll end up being Ethan the Spade soon enough."

Moving back into place to watch over the Princess, Stephan didn't want to tell Ethan what he suspected.

Slowly the food disappeared into hungry mouths. Drink was consumed by parched mouths. The orchestra slowed down and began to signal the start of the light show.

In small groups, people climbed up to the balconies in the trees that would provide the best vantage points to watch the light show.

One by one the lights began to dim and disappear before the fireflies started blinking their cues. Lights started appearing in the trees. Iridescent creatures lit up Mermaid Lagoon. The Pirates filled the skies with fireworks from foreign climes.

A sense of loneliness filled Gabby. She could feel her parents love as they held hands and watched the Festival of Lights. Gareth had wrapped his arms around Mary's waist; they looked as if they were keeping a secret.

She wished Ethan was with her.

Appearing out of nowhere, he wrapped his hand in hers.

Looking at him, tears beginning to blur her vision, she whispered, "Don't leave me again."

"I can't promise that," he responded, wishing he could say otherwise.

Slowly the fireworks faded as the Pirates lit the last ones. The fireflies quit blinking and the glowing creatures sunk back down into the depths.

All that was left was the lights in the trees and candles in windows as Jack disappeared back into the darkness.

"I'll always protect you," was the last thing she heard him whisper into her ear. "Always."

"Do you think she'll ever forget him?" the King asked his wife.

"No," Queen Alice sighed. "I don't think she's supposed to."

She didn't want to tell him that her own time was running out.

"Then we'll help them."

"Ethan Jack needs it." She left out, *Or Wonderland will flounder.* Shaking her head, Alice laughed when she remembered her own husband's reluctance to tie himself to Wonderland. "You weren't so eager to marry me yourself if I recall."

"I wasn't good enough for you," Traylor answered before kissing his wife on the forehead.

"Then why can't Ethan feel the same way?" Alice wondered aloud.

The King looked at his wife and thought about her question. "Good thing we have some time to wait out their battle of wills against Wonderland's magical will." He chuckled until he saw his wife's face. "How long?"

"I wish I knew."

Chapter 17

Over the past four years, Gabby tried her hardest not to notice Ethan in the background. It was more difficult than she expected.

When he was in Wonderland, she would see him around the village with a girl she knew was not his sister. This girl appeared thrilled to be seen on the arm of the Huntsman who had retrieved the Crown Princess, but everybody else shook their heads whenever they saw Jack watching the Princess.

When he was in the Enchanted Forest during his missions Gabby worried about his welfare. Would another Were find him and turn him into a Were-Huntsman in an attempt to create a Were-Army that would be used to destroy the kingdoms?

Even she had to admit that her imagination could get the best of her at times.

She still worried. Was he safe? Did he love that nameless villager? Did she ever cross his mind?

Weekly she waited for an announcement of his pending nuptials.

"Gabrielle!" her sister-in-law's voice echoed down the hallway. "I have news!"

She loved her brother's wife, Mary. Truly, she did. But the girl's combined innocence, enthusiasm, and maternal instincts annoyed her.

"In here," Gabby responded without moving from her spot on the window seat, the big book about budgeting lay across her lap.

"I have amazing news!" the tiny girl floated. "I am going to have a baby!"

"I bet Gareth is happy."

"He's over the moon happy," Mary beamed.

Pasting a weak smile on her face, Gabby whispered her congratulations to an excited and distracted Mary.

"I know that if the baby is a girl, I have to name her Wendy, but if the baby is a boy I'm leaning towards Peter or John.

She wondered if she would have married Ethan if his inner Jack had not taken over. Would they have their own little baby Alice right now if they had?

"I am so thankful that every other generation has to have an original name from their story as the heir's name…"

What would they have named a boy?

"…I am horrible at deciding names…"

Mary didn't notice when Gabby turned back to the window that faced the Enchanted Forest. It was in that direction that her heartstrings tugged.

Chapter 18

The announcement of the Wonderland Ball was circling the country. The Duchess of Hearts and the Duke of Diamonds started polishing their respected gemstones – rubies for the Duchess and diamonds for the Duke. The Red Duke and the Duchess of Spades started pulling out outfit after outfit. The Duke's wife longed to wear blue even though tradition would push her towards red. The Duchess' sons hoped that their mother wouldn't insist on her Spade shaped headdress – she would.

Above all else, these various Dukes and Duchesses – former kings and queens before Alice slew the Jabberwocky and was granted the ruling crown – crossed their fingers and toes in hope that it would be their son that caught the future Queen's eye. Even the Duchess of Clubs hoped that her youngest daughter would catch Princess Gabrielle's attention; it hardly mattered that Isabella Club was secretly engaged to the White Duke and Duchess' son, Fredrick.

In the town, the Hatters and the Hares were bustling about filling tea and cake orders. Their chatter was contagious and it made its way into the Retired Spade's home.

Jill, not caring that her brother was in residence, had burst into her parents' house with the news, "Princess Gabby is having a ball in order to find a husband!"

"Princess Gabrielle," her mother quietly corrected without looking up from her mending. "You can't keep referring to her informally in public."

"We aren't in public; we're at home," Jill protested, turning to look at her father. "She's told me that we are all invited, even the teenaged boys." Avoiding looking at her brother, "Everybody's talking about it. There are to be three balls, thanks to the tradition Cinderella started, and the first one is a masked ball. Even Ethan could dance with her that night and nobody but he would ever know." She started rattling off plans like the dress that her new best friend was going to let her borrow and how her mask was silver with blue accents.

But Ethan Jack tuned her out. Would he dare, he wondered, crash the Wonderland Balls just to dance with the fair princess? He couldn't get her out of his head no matter how many people he dated.

Would Gabby know that it was him?

"We must all wear blue," Jill insisted, "because all of the districts are wearing what is representative of their heads. Since we are part of the capital, we must wear blue somewhere on our attire."

Her mother started dreaming. It was at the last Wonderland Ball that she found her husband and decided to change her clubs for the royal color.

Chapter 19

Gabby wished to say that there was a wash of colors surrounding her. She missed seeing the daily pop of colors – greens and purples mostly – amongst the red, white, black, and blues scattered along the dance floor. White dresses were decorated with black clubs and red diamonds. Rubies and sapphires sparkled among the colorless diamonds and dark onyx worn by the party-goers. Gray dresses would be trimmed with black clubs or ribbons. Pale pink. Light blue. All signifying unmarried attendees.

Unmarried but not necessarily unattached.

Isabella Club was hidden in a corner with Fredrick White. Gabby had a suspicion that her friend would be eloping any day now while they were both in the same location. *Her mother will have a fit*, the Princess mused.

As often as she was passed around among her dance partners, Gabby was more thankful for the full year of dance lessons her mother had insisted on as a refresher course. If any toes were stepped on it was not because of her. Turns and spins were executed perfectly on her end. Deidrick Diamond did nearly stumble into her, but the princess suspected that Gregory Red had something to do with that mishap.

Diamond. Red. White. Club. Spade. Red. Club. Heart. So many sons angling for their chance at the throne, ignoring the gossip that the Princess had already lost her heart – and possibly her head – over a mere Huntsman.

So many alliances created and broken. The White Duchess was nearly heartbroken to find her son with a Club and stormed off to confront the Duchess of Clubs. The entire time the Black Duke and Duchess fumed in a corner, wishing that the Princess was a few years younger so that their own children would have been eligible for the marriage market. Nathan Black wished that his first wife had given him sons instead of daughters – all of who disappeared into other counties as soon as they turned of age to inherit their trust funds bestowed on them by their deceased mother. Madeline Black started putting into motion her plot to take over the throne, unbeknownst to her husband.

In a dark corner, observing the power-hungry Duchess, reclined a Huntsman in disguise. Sapphire and light blues mingled together enough to confuse the unmarried ladies of his attachment. Even the village girl he had been seeing for several months was confused by his attire and the fact that he had refused to escort her to the ball.

Looking over at the Card standing fifteen feet away from him, Jack casually signaled that they needed to be on the lookout. The Card, a Five of Hearts, nodded his head before speaking into a wireless device.

Remaining in the shadows, he continued to listen to Madeline Black telling her friends to stay away from the back and side doors. The refreshment table should be safe. The dance floor would be okay. When chaos would erupt, they needed to escape out of the front doors or the servants' entrance.

Maybe the Black Duchess had more planned than she led everybody to believe. Carefully, he observed names and faces. Even Nathan Black wasn't above Jack's observations; the clueless Duke might not have been aware of how far gone down the rabbit hole his current wife had gone, but he wasn't out of the loop either.

Even with watching the area, the explosion of activity still shocked Jack. He was aware, without a doubt, that he wouldn't reach the royal family in time. He could barely see his brothers surrounding the King and Queen, but he couldn't see the princess, the prince, or the prince's wife anywhere nearby.

A sudden scream, "Gabby!" got him running in the direction of Mary, Gareth's wife. Sobbing, the newly revealed to be expecting princess, cradled her husband to her chest. "Gareth," she cried, rocking back and forth. Looking up when Jack joined her side, "Is he going to be okay?"

The clash of metal against metal sounded near him, and Jack turned quickly, watching enthralled as Princess Gabrielle used her brother's ceremonial sword against the person who, Jack assumed, had attacked Gareth.

Checking her weak form and whistling to a nearby Card to help the princess, Jack crouched down to quickly examine the prince. Looking at the knot on Prince Gareth's forehead and the blood seeping from a wound on his shoulder, Jack shook his head at the sloppy work. "I need material for a bandage," he stated, not looking as Princess Mary quickly tore her petticoat. Something behind him had distracted him.

Squeaking, Gabby felt her exhaustion creeping up on her burst of adrenaline. Beginning to fear the worst, Jack interrupted her fight, "Help your brother," he growled. "Bandage his shoulder."

Stunned, she watched as he intercepted her opponent before his directive caught her attention. Jack would protect her. He always protected her. Spinning around, she caught Mary holding back her tears as blood began to trickle through a wound on Garth's shoulder. "Did it go all the way through?" she asked.

"I don't know. Here's the fabric Jack wanted." Mary's eyes moved frantically between Gareth and Jack.

"Push him up a little bit," Gabby commanded. "I'm not about to lose my brother after all these years." Channeling a first aide class she'd taken when she was fifteen and started to babysit, Gabby tore into Gareth's coat and shirt and examined the wound. "Just a flesh wound. He wasn't trying to kill Gareth."

But that comment made her realize that her opponent had been trying to kill her. Shaking the thought from her head, she felt Jack rejoining them. "Hold Gareth up," she instructed him. "Mary, hold his arm up." Carefully, she wrapped the makeshift bandage around her brother's shoulder, trying to get it wrapped tight but not too tight.

"Princess," Jack hissed to get her attention. "Where's the nearest escape tunnel from here?"

Looking up at Jack then at the chaos happening around them, Gabby paused in taking care of Gareth's shoulder. She couldn't see her parents. She couldn't even see where the refreshment table had been only minutes before. All she could see was Cards and Huntsmen battling men dressed in Black. Not even her parents were visible from where they had been previously sitting on their thrones.

No, what she saw was much worse.

"Princess!" Jack growled at her, trying to regain her attention.

Mary was the one who answered Jack's question. "It's behind the tapestry next to that column; the one with the white horse and the Jabberwocky."

Near the throne were Jack's brothers and the Cards forming a semi-circle around the King and Queen. She could see her mother sobbing, her blue dress covered in blood. Blood that was forming a huge circle, a circle growing by the second, on her father's chest.

"Princess!" Jack hissed, trying not to shout and draw attention to where they were at. The Cards nearest him were still battling the Black Duchess' men. "Princess."

"Gabby!" Mary growled. "Gareth needs to get out of here. I will not lose the father of my child." Poking her sister-in-law in the shoulder, she missed the sobbing coming from the throne. "Not now considering how many times we've tried and failed. I can't lose him too!"

Choking on the tears that refused to make it past her throat, Gabby turned away from where Jack's brothers were trying to protect the Queen. She allowed Mary to prod her towards the tapestry, not paying attention to if anybody was watching them. That was Jack's job.

Looking around them, Jack carefully lifted Gareth and looked around the room. He counted three brothers guarding a distraught queen. "Charlie," he whispered, recognizing which brother wasn't standing. Saying a quick prayer, he hurried the royals in his care into the hidden tunnel. Taking a quick glance around them, Jack made certain nobody, especially nobody in black, noticed their escape.

Darkness enclosed them as the hidden tunnel was closed and secured.

"The Queen and King will escape through the tunnel that is behind the thrones," Mary commented.

It was that simple comment that made Princess Gabrielle break down into tears just as Mary was beginning to calm down.

"What did I say?" Mary asked, bewildered.

Jack carefully lowered Prince Gareth to the floor before searching the walls for the hidden lights that were supposed to be put in place before the Ball just in case of situations like this happened. He didn't know if they would be battery-operated flashlights or match-lit torches.

Taking a deep breath, Jack answered her as soon as he grasped on the hidden cache of flashlights. "The King was attacked; he didn't make it." Letting out a breath, "And we need to get out of here before anybody can break down," he sternly told the Princesses. "I promise, Princess," he lowered himself to Gabby's level, "you'll have your chance to break down. Just not right now."

"Where are we going to go?" she whispered.

"Neverland," Mary answered her.

"No," Jack answered. "That's the first place the Black Duchess' men will look for you, Prince Gareth, and the Princess." Taking another deep breath, "We have to get lost in the Enchanted Forest."

Chapter 20

Escaping the Castle was easier than it should have been. While the Duchess had been able to pull off a coup d'état for the history books, everything had not been planned down to the smallest detail. She hadn't been expecting that the Prince and Princess would be able to escape. None of her soldiers had been aware of the hidden tunnels that aided in the Princess's escape.

"Where would she go?" the enraged Duchess screamed.

Refusing to show any emotion, even loss at the murder of her husband, the Queen merely shrugged what she could of her shoulders. "How should I know? I can't track my children."

Pushing a branding iron into a brazier, the red-headed Duchess turned to face the eerily calm Alice. "Tell me."

"Madeline, if I knew I still wouldn't tell you."

Letting out a roar of outrage, the Duchess shoved the hot end of the branding iron into the Queen's exposed shoulder. The Queen stoically took the iron burning her flesh without a sound.

Turning her head to look at the mark, Alice calmly responded. "I should have known you were a Heart. Your hair is red and your family has also been emotional and blood-thirsty. However," the Queen serenely smiled, "none of them have ever decided to destroy the foundation of Wonderland before."

"Wonderland will be better off with me as its Queen," she answered while pressing the iron against the Queen's forehead. "Why won't you cry?" she poked the Queen a few more times with the iron.

"I have no reason to. You weren't clever. We knew this day would come. My daughter is safe."

Face turning red, the Duchess screeched, "Off with her head!" Yanking the Queen by her hair, she added, "Call all the townspeople to an assembly."

Queen Alice the Fifth coolly announced, "The Jabberwocky will be coming soon."

They hid in the back rooms of Liny's tea shoppe while they waited to see what the aftermath was going to be. Would her mother go Queen of Hearts on The Black Duchess and her followers? Was her mother even okay?

Several times Madeline Hatter slipped into the room, shaking her head as more and more rumors raced through the town. Whispering something in Jack's ear, she shook her head sadly before leaving the room.

"What's wrong?" Mary whispered to him, careful not to disturb where Gareth's was resting. She was constantly touching her husband to check his fever.

Closing his eyes, Jack informed them of the one thing he had hoped wasn't true. "My brother Charlie didn't survive his injuries." He wondered how Henry was going to reorganize the Cards. He worried about Charlie's wife and three sons.

Leaning against the wall, Gabby spoke up. None of them were aware that she was awake. "Does that mean you'll be a Spade or a Club?"

Mary looked at the two of them carefully until Jack explained, "My mother built in a replacement system. Stephan the Spade could become the Club if Henry decrees it. Derek then would become the Spade and I'd become a diamond. Henry could also change Stephan to the Club and use my middle made to make me a Spade so that Derek can remain a Diamond. Although, Henry being the Heart is also likely to lead using his heart and make a smoother transition of turning me into a Club." Closing his eyes, "Either way, Charlie's children will keep their Card standings."

"Jack," Gabrielle whispered, "You aren't a Huntsman anymore." He understood the royal command beneath her words.

The other meaning behind her comment was that Cards did not marry into the Royal family. Closing her eyes again, Gabby pushed back the fresh round of tears that threatened to escape. She never expected everything to fall apart so spectacularly.

The deciding factor in their plans happened when a miserable Liny slipped back into the backroom for the final time.

"What is it, Liny?" Mary whispered.

"Madeline, please," Liny whispered. She felt uncomfortable being informal with the Royals because of their current situations. "The Black Duchess has overthrown the crown. Ethan's brothers are now tossed in the dungeon to await a test of their loyalty. I think they are hoping that the Cards will reveal how Ethan and the surviving members of the royal family have escaped." Turning towards Princess Gabrielle, "Your Majesty," she whispered, "The Black Duchess executed your mother during a public assembly and has a reward out for your capture. Dead or Alive." Closing her eyes, "She's sending people to Neverland to search for Princess Mary and Prince Gareth. She knows that any child that the princess is carrying could become the monarch of two kingdoms if Princess Gabby…" she paused, "I'm sorry, the Queen cannot be located. Logically she knows that she cannot be crowned until the Queen and her siblings can be located."

"I am not Queen yet. There hasn't been a coronation," Gabby weakly protested.

Jack was the first person to notice that Madeline was changing titles. Jack was no longer Jack because he was no longer a Huntsman. Princess Gabrielle was no longer the princess; she was now the uncrowned Queen of Wonderland.

As the closest Card, he was now her advisor, much like his father was towards her dearly departed mother."

"I'm not ready to be queen," Gabby whispered. "I just want to be Princess Gabby, not Queen Gabrielle. I want my father back. I want Charlie back; he told the best jokes and helped me escape that odious history tutor." Breaking down, she reached for the closest person – Ethan.

"Your Majesty," he whispered, pulling her close, "We need to get out of Liny's shop. The Duchess is going to search everywhere shortly and we need to be over the Bridge before she gets close. She'll have no problem destroying anybody found helping you."

Mary added, "We need to get Gareth to safety too."

Pulling back, Gabby looked over at Liny. Remembering the disguise her friend, Pamina frequently used, she stated, "I need a tin of unpackaged black tea and that black tea and raspberry blend. And hot water." Madeline was almost to the door before Gabby remembered to add, "And that bag that I dropped off here weeks ago." Turning towards Ethan, "You need to carefully cut off all decorations from your coat and put it over Gareth's shirt. We'll take the medals and buttons with us so that nobody can find them." Turning towards Mary, "We need to get out of our dresses. I'll have something you can fit into."

She didn't tell Mary that they were going to be wearing pants or that the tea was to dye their hair. Gabby also didn't warn Mary before she cut off the girl's waist-length hair above the shoulders. Closing her eyes, she did the same thing to her own hair.

Minutes later Madeline returned with the items, a frantic light beginning to form in her eyes. Without saying anything, she turned towards Mary to help her dye her hair. Gabby pulled out the pants and shirt and handed them over to Mary before grabbing her own pair. Stuffing her dress into the bag, she held it out for the pieces that Ethan had cut off of his coat.

"Take this and dye Gareth's hair, will you?" she asked Ethan before grabbing some of the paste and rubbing it into her own hair. She hoped that the raspberry in the tea would help put some red highlights into their hair.

The only thing the new queen felt like she could do while her world was falling apart was to try to keep what remained of it together.

Chapter 21

The cold reality overwhelmed Gabby. She was no longer Princess Gabby and that knowledge terrified her. She wasn't ready to assume the throne. She didn't even have a clue on how to regain her throne.

The clang of swords still echoed in her ears. She could still feel the tacky blood that had slowly seeped from her brother's wound. How was the dethroned princess supposed to take charge? Instead, she started shaking.

"Gabby," Ethan murmured.

Ethan, she thought. He could no longer be Jack. Jack was a Huntsman. Ethan was her Spade.

"Spade," she declared him, ignoring the fact that it was actually Henry who would decide Ethan's suit. But his father had been a Spade and that Spade had been the Queen's Advisor, even after he retired. Drawing a deep breath, "What do I do?" she asked him.

"Get Gareth and Mary secure," he informed her. "If something happens to Mary then Neverland will declare war against us and that's the last thing we need."

Blinking, she looked at him, an idea forming. "You mean Neverland declares war against the Black Duchess…"

Looking at her, Ethan could see the strategist behind her eyes. "What do you need?"

"A secure place and a Huntsman." With that statement, the future queen began to plot.

"I don't understand," the Black Duchess cried. "The people hate me."

Her husband rolled his eyes before commenting, "Well, you did behead the beloved Queen, imprison all of the Cards who protected the town, and banish the missing Princess."

"I freed everybody."

A Card chained against the wall gave a cold laugh, "You destroyed us all."

"Hush, peasant," she commanded, signaling to a soldier to reap more abuse on the Card.

The Red Duke, caged in another corner, joined in, feeling emboldened after watching the Heart speak up. "He's right."

Turning towards the caged dissenters, the Duchess looked at the battered red that the Red Duke, the Red Duchess, and the Duchess of Hearts wore. Red blood stains were turning brown.

"Bring me the Red Duke's children!"

"You'll bring the Jabberwocky to us!" another Card voiced. "And nobody except the Rightful Queen knows where the sword is hidden."

"The Jabberwocky is a myth."

"The Jabberwocky is real!" The Red Duke voiced, not caring that three soldiers approached him. He only had himself to lose, secure in knowing that his children were well hidden. "Read the legends. Go to the center of Wonderland where nothing will grow generations later!"

His wife screamed as her husband disappeared under the soldiers. "If you want Wonderland to love you then you cannot rule with fear."

There were more voices against her than there were Knights. The only thing that kept the Cards, Reds, Hearts, Diamonds, and Spades from rising up were the cages where she had secured them.

"Has anybody found the Clubs yet?"

Nobody wanted to tell her that they were hiding Charlie's body from her abuse or had managed to escape in an attempt to find the Royal Siblings.

"If Princess Mary is hurt," Henry rasped, "then Neverland will declare war against Wonderland and your soldiers cannot hold them back." He grunted when the nearest soldier struck him in the gut, but it was nothing compared to what he felt when the Queen had been tortured before the Duchess had called for her execution.

"When the Huntsmen learn about Charlie and Jack, they will declare war against you," the Spade she never could remember his name, added. He held back his groans at the soldiers attacked.

"And," the Diamond added, "even if you can defeat Neverland, the Huntsmen, and the Loyal Wonderlandians, you still have to single-handedly defeat the Jabberwocky."

"The Jabberwocky is a legend!" The Black Duchess screamed while her soldiers bruised the Head Cards. "Take them to the dungeons with the other Cards!"

Chapter 22

Groaning, Gareth mumbled something about portals while Ethan tried to carry the Prince.

"Portals?" Gabby asked, turning towards Mary.

Releasing a sigh, the other Princess looked at her husband. "When we married a portal between Neverland and Wonderland was secured in an undisclosed location. There is one hidden in both palaces and only Gareth and I know where they are located."

Hefting Gareth up, Ethan added, "And the Card who set it up." He was increasingly tempted to leave the wounded Prince exactly where he was; throwing him over his shoulder like a sack of potatoes was out of the question thanks to Gareth's wound.

Mary blinked as she scanned her memory. "His bodyguard."

"Then the portal should be safe," Ethan whispered. "Nobody can reveal its location now." He didn't want to tell them that with Charlie's death it was likely that the portal no longer existed.

Reestablishing a link between the two allied kingdoms would be next on the things to fix as soon as Gabby was crowned. In a few months, neither girl would be able to take the time for a lengthy trip.

"Let's stop here for the night," he said instead.

Gabby had been quiet since his comment. "It was Charlie, wasn't it?"

"Yes."

"And he's dead."

"Yes."

"So, the portal is gone." Pausing, "And Gareth doesn't know." Looking at her brother's motionless body, "He doesn't know any of it."

The place he had stopped them wasn't ideal. A covering of pine trees kept them from being seen, but the sap, pine needles, and pine cones found themselves into uncomfortable places. Gabby was aware that, ever since they passed over the Wonderland Bridge, it was up to the Enchanted Forest to guide their path.

"Please let us find help for my brother," was her constantly whispered prayer. She hoped that the powers-that-be would hear her pleas. They couldn't continue on like they were doing.

"Princess," Ethan started while he distractedly tried to settle Gareth in place.

"Yes," Gabby and Mary both answered him.

Looking at the girls, he started over, "Gabby, you know how this place works."

"Right," she whispered before closing her eyes. A pile of pillows and blankets appeared next to a picnic basket filled with food.

Eyes wide, "How did you do that?" Mary asked.

"Magic," Gabby answered simply. "It is the Enchanted Forest after all."

They saw her pause before leaping on the basket. Pulling out sandwiches and drinks, Gabby kept digging. Finally, a small white box with a red cross on the top was pulled out from the bottom of the basket. "Yes!" she almost shouted.

Moving closer to her brother, the Princess popped open the lid. Digging through it, she handed a small towel to Mary. "Get this wet with the clear liquid in that bottle."

"That's just water," Mary stated, puzzled until she opened the bottle. "Wow! That's some strong stuff!"

"It'll help stop the infection," Gabby whispered as she took the towel back. "Pull his shirt up," she instructed Ethan before cleaning the wound. She was more than thankful that her brother had already passed out.

Digging through the box, Mary saw items she couldn't understand including needles and thick black thread.

"There's a yellow tube of antibiotic ointment in there."

"This?" Mary asked, holding up the wrong item.

"No, the other one." Taking it from her sister-in-law, Gabby smeared it on Gareth. Turning to Ethan she asked, "How are you at making stitches?"

"Decent. Why?"

"Take the needle, the shallow bowl, and that clear liquid. Put both of them in the bowl." Gabby instructed, thinking about her emergency first aid classes from when she was fifteen.

"Cut a length of the thread and carefully close Gareth up." In a whisper, she weakly added, "If I see any more blood I will be passing out."

Distracting Mary with the food, Gabby cleaned her hands before digging in. "Ethan should be done soon. It's only five stitches."

"Where did you learn this?"

"My adoptive family. My... Preston wanted me prepared when I decided to start babysitting to earn extra money."

Shaking her head, Mary sighed, "I always wished that my mother had fostered me out, but she never had any more children after me."

"It isn't as great as you would think. Coming here was a huge shock. I let Ethan ramble about all kinds of boring things when I first found myself in the Enchanted Forest." Gabby smiled at the memory.

Hiding was the easy part. No matter how many soldiers passed them nobody turned to spot them. There were a few times where Ethan would have sworn that they had been seen, but the beleaguered soldiers would continue walking.

It puzzled him until Gabby witnessed it. "She has their fear, but not their loyalty," she explained in a whisper. "The Duchess can tell them to do something or risk their heads.

That doesn't mean that they have to do more than the basic commands."

"Why?" Mary whispered.

"Things are different than Neverland. You have four or five kingdoms and sometimes loyalty shifts. There's only one kingdom in Wonderland. These people have seen brothers, sisters, cousins, family members destroyed at her hands. Maybe their lives or families are threatened. Maybe…"

Ethan interrupted Gabby, "Maybe they see you as hope."

Turning to look at him, she asked, "Hope?"

"You never threatened, injured, or killed them. Last year a story circulated about an orphan you helped."

"I did what anybody else would do."

"But not everybody would," Mary interjected. "Gareth told me that story. You provided food for those siblings until you could find a family that would take both of them."

Turning to stare at the Neverland Princess, Ethan stated, "I never even heard that story. My orphan was the one she gave a job to."

Gabby sat there staring at them. It never occurred to her that there were people who would refuse to help others. It wasn't the orphans' fault that their parents had died.

"It's the Royal family's responsibility to help out," she stated.

Mary looked at where Gareth was resting and snorted. "Right. Every month Gareth gives money to the charitable organizations that normally handle those sorts of things."

"It isn't always wise to be so hands-on, Your Majesty," Ethan calmly added. "There's a school that handles the children."

Sitting up straight, she declared, "When we get back to Wonderland, we will be checking out this 'school' you speak of." Her tone was powerful enough for Ethan the Spade to take notice and sit up straighter.

"We?"

"You are my Spade," was all she said before magicking up a picnic basket.

He was her bodyguard. It took Ethan more time than necessary to connect those dots about why she had declared him the Spade.

The Spade protected the princess and he was the only Card available.

He just didn't understand that by naming him as her Spade she was also keeping him close. She was willing to play a long game in order for him to see reason.

Gabby had learned that much while playing chess with her father.

Chapter 23

The days of ball gowns and everyday dresses were behind her. Pulling on a pair of boy's trousers, Gabby girded her loins towards the battle that was soon to come. She had read books and watched movies about war, about fighting, about manipulative tactics. She just had no practical knowledge.

"Quick shaking," Ethan shouted at her. "You are just as likely to take off your own head as you are your opponents."

Sword fighting lessons weren't going as smoothly as either of them had initially anticipated. Her parents had never suspected that she would need them and Gabby suspected she would have figured out how to skip the lessons based on how badly she was currently doing.

"Posture," he shouted at her. "Mind your balance!"

"I'm trying!" Gabby shouted back at him.

"Don't drop your guard!"

Charging over from where Mary and Gareth were watching the Princess's lesson, Mary snatched the sword from Gabby's hands and faced off against Ethan. "Watch and learn," she stated.

"Be careful," Gareth warned her from the sidelines where he was recovering.

Ethan looked at Gareth before stating, "I know about the baby," he reassured the Prince of Wonderland and Princess of Neverland's Consort.

Mary shook her head and hissed, "Gabby isn't concentrating because she is fighting against you." Turning to face her sister-in-law, "Pay attention."

Step-by-step she gave Gabby some simple pointers without breathing heavily. "Step One, Gabby, is to trust your gut." Turning elaborately, she spun around a tree, "Step two is to be aware of your surroundings. Trees. Stairs. Balconies. Places where you can trap and be trapped."

"Also, the lighting in the room," Ethan added. "Darkness can conceal you or your opponent just as light can reveal."

"Or blind," Gareth added, remembering a fight he had where the bright sun in front of him both blinded him and blurred his opponent's movements.

"Be prepared to engage before you engage," Mary added. "Drawing your sword takes precious moments and can give your opponent an advantage." She nimbly leaped onto a rock and looked down at where Ethan was staring at her. "Also, guard your position. Right here, Ethan can attack my ankles and I don't have the best defense against him."

Gareth chuckled as Mary gracefully jumped down and reengaged Ethan in swordplay. "And relax. Your movements will be jerky and that could end up being your downfall. Being able to go with the flow means you'll be able to better anticipate your opponent's movements."

"Balance," Ethan reminded her. "Always try to keep your balance." Shaking his head, "And I don't think that I need to remind you again to be careful with your sword." He was trying to figure out how Mary still wasn't having trouble breathing and he was starting to become short of breath.

Gareth chuckled from where he was watching them, "Before we found out she was expecting, Mary practiced daily with either her father's soldiers or my father's soldiers." He left out that it had been a distraction from the children that would never be.

"They never learned step seven. They need to have a good defense and they lowered it because they didn't want to hurt a Crown Princess." Mary spun around quickly and managed to disarm Ethan. "And it's a great idea to remain confident."

"Keep your arms out and elbows in."

"Keep your weapon at the ready. You have to anticipate whatever could happen."

Gabby kept looking between the trio as they continued to instruct her, showing her positions and techniques. Eventually, she took the sword back from Mary and faced Ethan. "Okay, I'm ready now."

"Don't touch that!" Gabby shouted as her brother started to reach through a cluster of plants with clusters of three leaves. "Haven't you ever seen poison ivy before?"

Drawing back, Gareth flushed at her words. "No."

"Well if you are anything like me, you'll break out in an itchy, blistery rash that won't go away for weeks. We can't afford that."

"But my dagger," he protested.

Closing her eyes, Gabby pictured the dagger on a towel. "We'll wash it off when we reach a stream," she told him as she carefully folded it up in the towel before wrapping the bundle up in a second towel. "Better safe than sorry," she added before handing it over to Ethan for safekeeping.

"How do you know I'm not allergic to that plant?" he asked.

"Are you?"

"No."

"Okay then."

She couldn't explain how she already knew that he wasn't allergic to poison ivy. Gabby knew that they wanted an explanation, but giving it to them would only cause even more questions.

Even she couldn't explain why she suddenly knew things.

Like Gareth's extreme dislike of strawberries.

Or that Mary lied when she said she didn't like them, but actually loved them. She would sneak them in the middle of the night when Gareth was asleep.

It's how she knew that Gareth would have a severe allergic reaction. His face would swell up and he would be unable to breathe. Her brother would slowly and painfully suffocate to death all because he would touch his hand to his face.

"How did you know I could be allergic to that plant?" Gareth asked his sister.

"I had a serious reaction one time. I only touched a tiny little plant, but it spread nearly everywhere. The doctor said that if it had spread to my face when I'd first made contact with the plant that I could have suffocated." Gabby fudged the truth a bit. "We have the same parents so there are very good odds that you are just as allergic as I am." She couldn't tell him that his allergic reaction would be worse than her reaction in front of Mary. "I needed a shot and I don't think that the Forest can magic one of those up."

The title of Queen kept her tossing and turning throughout the nights. She knew that she had yet to be crowned, but it was understood amongst the foursome. Her brother said nothing, knowing that he was technically the Crown Prince just in case something happened to his sister.

Screams ripped through the air as the nightmare of what her parents must have endured played itself through her imagination, filtering into her dreams. Madeline Hatter had told her nothing, but Gabby knew that the Black Duchess would have made it a public execution.

She would have the Queen dressed up in her finest gown – the dark blue one with black and red suits adorning the hem. Her mother's blonde hair would have been finely done as to keep the hair off of her neck.

No, the Duchess knew what she was doing. Her fiery red hair would be just as elaborately done as the Queen's hair. Her gown would be a brilliant Red with tiny black hearts scattered around the dress. A little unknown fact was that the Black Duke's second wife had lied about her origins; Madeline Black, originally Madeline Heart Mason, was a descendant of the infamous Queen of Hearts.

And still, the dreams of her mother's torture kept appearing days later, dreams that were filled with information and gruesome images that could only be true.

Sitting up, gasping for air as she tried to force the image of her mother's head rolling across the makeshift platform, Gabby allowed the tears to fall from her face. Saying nothing, Ethan climbed into the make-shift bed and pulled her into his arms.

She couldn't tell him that she knew the exact minute her mother had been murdered. A rush of magic so potent had rushed into her body, causing her to stumble around as if in a drunken stupor for a few minutes as it situated itself into her body. Gabby knew that Ethan knew nothing about the magical bond she now shared with the throne and with Wonderland – it was a well-kept secret.

"Shh," he whispered while rocking her back and forth in his arms. "It will be okay. It will be fine. It was just a dream."

But she couldn't tell him that it wasn't just a dream. These visions weren't something she would ever be able to easily forget.

Chapter 29

Pacing in front of the cage where the three brothers had been imprisoned, the Duchess glared at them each in turn.

"Where are the other Clubs?" had been asked so many times they could hear her words in their sleep – as limited as it was.

The Diamond, nursing an untreated broken arm and barely checked rage, only glared at her. Derek doubted that she would like his answer anyway if his arm was any indicator.

The Spade smirked. He knew where they were because the Princess was still alive. She might not be aware that their small group was being followed, but he knew it because of their connection. He could track her and know if she was being followed thanks to his bodyguard magic. And if the Duchess did know where the Princess was then she would also know where the nine missing Clubs were hiding.

He hated that he was the only Card who still had a connection to one of the Royals. Not counting Ethan who was now either a Spade or a Club. They wouldn't know until the Princess was found or Henry declared Ethan's suit.

Then Stephan would be the Club and he would be able to find the missing Clubs, but no official changes had been made.

The Heart, however, glared. He had watched his Queen tortured before she was beheaded. He had felt every single scalding poker and branding iron. He had felt the medieval torture devices slowly pull at the Queen's limbs as she stoically remained silent. He had felt the blade slice through her neck.

His brothers could attest that it hadn't been so easy for the Heart. Henry felt it all and continued to suffer for it.

"Your men killed the only Card who could have answered that question," he snarled. I can tell you that Hearts Two, Five, Six, and Nine are in Cell Number Thirty-Seven. Three and Four are in the water torture tank. Seven and Eight are dead." He said the last two sadly. These were his cousins. These were his friends. These were children who were too young to be tortured so maliciously. Someday those numbers could have been his children.

Derek spoke up. "Diamonds Two and Nine are with your husband. Three, Eight, and..." he paused, "Four are in

Cell Number Four, but Four is about to die from his untreated wound. Five is in the water tank. Seven is dead."

The Spade added, "Spades Two, Five, Seven, and Nine are dead. Two and Seven were shot in the back by your cowards as they tried to escape to find the Princess. They were murdered near the Observation Tower when your men shot them in the back. Five was run through with a sword and died in the ballroom. Nine was slowly burned alive by your hand while his brothers watched." He paused, but only Henry noticed it. "Three and Four are with five of your missing soldiers. Six and nine are in Cell Number Five."

The Duchess straightened up; her motions too jerky to cover up her surprise. Turning around abruptly, she left the brothers alone.

"Missing soldiers?" Henry whispered.

"Lies. Three and Four are with the Clubs," he barely breathed loud enough for Henry to hear. "They found the Princess."

"Good," Derek groaned. "And the Duchess will drive herself crazy trying to figure out who is missing."

Smirking, "Never question a soldier's loyalty. It's one of the easiest ways to get them to turn on you."

Pacing back and forth –characteristic observers quickly noticed the Duchess had whenever she was frustrated – she scanned her assembled ranks. There were too many gaps for her to rest assured that everybody was accounted for.

"He's guarding the Cards."

"He fell in the Ballroom Battle."

"He's guarding the dungeon."

They were all reasons, not a single excuse, and everything the ranks told her could be confirmed, but the ranks could tell that she still didn't believe them by the barrage of questions she bombarded them with after they had answered her initial question.

They started to shift in place, wondering what their leader was thinking.

This uncomfortable shifting was attributed to guilt and she pointed towards one of the youngest, and more fidgety, soldiers.

"I don't believe any of you," she announced to the frozen room. "I'll just have to show you what your guilt will get you." Motioning to her bodyguard for the ax he carried, she took a swing.

The front row stood stock still as the young boy's head rolled towards them. His father's agonized cries echoed throughout the room as the Duchess handed the ax back to the dumbfounded bodyguard.

Blood splattered on her face, she stared at her men. "Report any traitors or face the consequences." Sweeping away from the soldiers, the Duchess demanded that somebody clean up the 'mess' in the ballroom and for a bath.

She never noticed the father that now mourned for his sixteen-year-old son or the exchange of looks between many of the men.

"My Dear," the Duke calmly started to say while staring at the pink water in the tub, "fear is not the best way to rule."

Staring at his reflection in the mirror, she snorted. "What do you, my dimwitted husband, know? You didn't even know I was planning this coupe. I married you for your money and you married me for the chance to have your sons."

Dismissing him, she started talking to her maid. She'd chosen this one very carefully from the Wonderland servants and if Marie considered pulling the Duchess's hair a few times nobody would have blamed her.

"What would your former master have to say?"

"The Queen would have agreed with your husband," she meekly answered, taking extra care to not pull on any strand of hair too tightly right then.

Glaring at Marie, she stated, "I am the Queen!"

A snort from her bodyguard came from the doorway. "Wonderland disagrees."

"I don't care what the people think."

"I'm not talking about the people."

The Duchess snorted her dismissal.

All the bodyguard said before blending into the background was, "The Jabberwocky is coming."

"The Jabberwocky isn't real!" she shouted to the empty room.

Jerking upright from her disturbing dream, Gabby gasped for breath. The Clubs she wasn't supposed to be aware of stirred restlessly in their hiding places. The two Spades were hidden in the trees and pulling guard duty.

"What is it?" Ethan asked, only aware of the Spades in the trees.

"The Clubs are guarding my brother," she whispered. "How much further until we reach Neverland?"

"Hopefully we will be there tomorrow afternoon." He knew that they had taken enough time that the Duchess' guards would have stopped watching for them, if they ever had been looking for the Royal Siblings.

"Good," Gabby sighed. "The Jabberwocky is coming."

Shaking his head, Ethan whispered, "You can't be serious. You don't even know where the Vorpal Blade is located.

Rolling her eyes, Gabby leaned towards her new Spade, "I've learned so many things ever since my mother lost her head. I must defeat the Jabberwocky with the Vorpal Blade and I know exactly where it is located."

"We just got you out of Wonderland."

"And I am refusing to let *that* Duchess keep me away from my home. I've lost too much to hand over my birthright to a power-mad descendant of the Queen of Hearts."

Chapter 25

The soldiers were split into two ranks: the willing and the unwilling.

The willing were those who had joined the Duchess from the beginning. She assumed she was secure with their undying loyalty, but she took too many things for granted.

The unwilling were the townspeople and the Cards she had taken prisoner. These were the people she threatened, chained, caged, and tortured in a misguided attempt to win their loyalty through fear tactics.

The willing witnessed her bloodthirsty actions and started to get nervous.

"Why?" was whispered around.

Why did she behead Ben?

Why did we join her forces?

"What?" soon joined the ever-growing list of why questions.

What do we do?

What can we do?

Finally, somebody leaned forward and stated what others were too scared to say.

"We release the cards."

The ranks of originally forty Cards were greatly diminished. All the Clubs and two of the Spades were still missing. Many of them didn't survive the Water Tank.

"Will they trust us?"

"Probably not and we'll have to watch out for the faithful, but if we can all escape…"

"Escape where?"

"We have to find the Princess."

Gabby stared out at the trees, lost in thought. She knew the Clubs would protect Gareth until they reached Neverland and the Lost Boys would then take over. They had already sent Two and Three off to warn Neverland about what happened and what might soon happen.

"I need to go back," she whispered. "I need to protect my land and not my brother."

"I know," Ethan resignedly whispered from where he'd been pretending to sleep.

"The Clubs will get them there."

"I know."

"And then they can spread out through Wonderland and find out what is in the other districts."

"I know."

"And I have three Spades to protect me."

"I know."

"Can't you say anything else?" Gabby hissed.

Ethan sat up and looked at her. "I'm agreeing with you."

"Well stop it!"

Chuckling, he moved to where he was sitting beside her. "Princess, you can't have it both ways."

"Fine. Okay. How do we get in?"

"Piece of cake."

Releasing the Jacks wasn't an easy task. They knew the Diamond had a broken arm; one of their own had been forced to give it to him. That didn't mean they weren't still nervous. The Jacks could easily overtake them even with their injuries. All that mattered was freeing the Cards; without them, the master plan would fail.

That still didn't mean that the carefully thought out plan didn't have its own share of risks and obstacles.

The biggest obstacle being that the Duchess spent so much time pacing in front of the Jacks' cage demanding answers that the brothers couldn't give her. Their answers never changed and it infuriated her even more.

What surprised everybody was when her head bodyguard drew her away from the Jacks. With a wink at the soldiers who were attempting to hide, he led the Duchess far away.

"But I'm not done interrogating them!" she whined.

"You wanted me to tell you when the Storybook Delegation was due to arrive. Don't want them to see you covered in dungeon dirt. They are already concerned about the areas of drought that are forming near the rivers."

"Nosy busybodies," the Duchess mumbled. "I wish Marie told me where the royal crowns are stored. These Jacks are useless." Lifting her nose in the air, the Duchess flounced off towards her bedroom calling for her bath to be ready when she got there.

"You have ten minutes," one of the Duchess' bodyguards hissed while the Duchess made her grand exit. "Guard has the keys."

The soldiers looked at each other. Was this a trap? Why was the bodyguard willing to help them?

"Ben was his brother," somebody remembered. The other soldiers went silent before they moved into action.

Sending somebody to distract Guard, a few others went to sneak up behind him and get the keys. A few of the lock pickers started to fiddle with the Jacks' cage. Nobody wanted to waste time or wait for the others to return with the keys.

There was no Storybook Delegation. At least not one that was scheduled to arrive. The group of seven was too nervous about getting trapped in Wonderland to actually venture beyond its bridge.

It was a ruse to get Gabby back into Wonderland Castle.

Looking at her identification, the gatekeeper on duty wondered if Mary Lennox was actually standing in front of him.

Ethan was tempted to punch the guard in the face because of the guard's skeptics. He also couldn't believe that he had passed as Jack from Jack and the Beanstalk.

"Have the others arrived yet?" he asked, trying to distract the gatekeeper. "Roschen and Schnee were both sending people. I think Rose and Snow themselves volunteered to be part of the Storybook Delegation. Or maybe it was their daughters. I never could keep track of which Princess was on the council when there were Princesses on the council.

"You are the first to arrive," the guard stated without looking up from the magically forged identification card.

"Typical. Princesses are always late," Ethan huffed. He didn't even grunt when Gabby elbowed him in the side.

Another guard entered the booth and glanced at Gabby. His eyes widened for a moment before he recovered. "What are you doing?"

"I can't tell if this is fake or not."

"Let me see it." Taking the card from the other guard's hand, he shook his head. "Good grief, boy. Why are you keeping the head of the Storybook Delegation waiting? Go on through, Ms. Lennox."

Princess Gabby and Ethan hurried through the gates before either guard changed their minds.

"What are you trying to do, Ernest, lose your head? If Ms. Lennox complained to the Duchess, I mean Queen of Hearts, then you could be headless like Ben right now!"

Ethan looked back at the gate. Suddenly he understood the first guard's hesitation and the second guard's wink. The ranks were scared or revolting. It would be interesting to discover how many soldiers were in either camp.

"What was that about?" Gabby mouthed back.

"The Duchess is losing her ranks," he whispered in response. "Come on. We still have to get to my brothers.

Leading the way, he skirted around the Castle entryway and towards the Library.

"Where are we going?"
"There are tunnels everywhere that only the Cards are aware of. Occasionally a Royal will discover them or know about them, like the ones in the Ballroom, but they are always in the company of a Card."
"Pushing her behind a white rose bush that looked as if it had been crudely painted red, Ethan looked around him before tapping on a brick.

"How?"

"Wonderland magic."

"Of course."

Taking a moment to orient himself to their location, he waited until their eyes had adjusted before explaining. "That way leads to a tunnel that will take you to the Throne Room. At the end of the tunnel, turn left and it'll take you straight there. A right will take you outside." He knew she needed to get the Vorpal Sword and wasn't willing to have another argument about it being quicker if they split up. "I'll meet you right here after I free my brothers."

"That's the plan," Gabby agreed before slipping into the dark.

He hoped he'd see her again.

Ethan was attempting to slip into the dungeon when his brothers and the other Cards came running up the stairs.

"It's a long story," Stephan grinned. Suddenly he took a step backward until he bumped into Henry. "I see, the Princess made you her Spade."

Pushing past his brothers, Henry calmly stated, "That makes things easier on me. Where are Stephan's Clubs?"

Nobody noticed Stephan stiffening up at Henry's pronouncement. Closing his eyes, he felt around for the connections that had just vanished. He couldn't feel any of them anymore. Not the other Spades. Not the Clubs Henry had just given him control over. Definitely not the Princess.

"They are with the Crown Prince. He needed to go to Neverland for medical attention. We had to be careful about moving him. The Princess instructed them to return and scout out the other districts when they get back to Wonderland. The Lost Boys will get the Prince to the castle once they reach the Neverland Bridge."

"Good. We need to know how far the Duchess's poison has spread and how much of it is based on fear."

Stephan looked around them before asking, "Where's the Princess?"

Tilting his head, Ethan eyed his brother before slowly stating, "With the Spades that found us."

"That doesn't help!" the bodyguard growled. "I can't feel any of them anymore. I haven't been able to ever since Henry unofficially made me a Club a few moments ago. I can't even feel the Clubs because they're in Neverland!"

"She's trying to break into the Throne Room," Ethan hissed, looking at the Duchess's soldiers while he answered Stephan.

Chuckling, Derek eased his brother's mind. "They let us out. There are about fifteen soldiers who are still on the Duchess's side and they are always with her. Her head bodyguard keeps moving them around so she doesn't notice that…"

"Off with her head!" bounced and echoed off the walls, sending the Jacks and their Cards sprinting towards the Throne Room.

Sneaking into the Throne Room was easy. A quick scan of the room led the Princess to the crest with two crossed swords situated over the throne.

"Clever, Mother," she whispered. "Now how do I get the swords down?"

Instinct told her it was one of the two practice-looking swords attached to the crest. Closing her eyes, Gabby wondered how she was supposed to get them down. Her mind's eye saw her levitating.

"Okay then."

Moving into position underneath the crest, she closed her eyes once again before feeling her feet leaving the floor. Visualizing what she wanted to happen, Gabby's concentration broke when the Duchess shouted, "Off with her head!"

Falling ten or twelve feet, they all heard the clatter and resulting echo of the crest hitting the floor.

"Well, aren't you a bloodthirsty wench," Gabby quipped as she carefully inched towards the crest. One of those swords was the Vorpal Blade and she needed to get her hands on the swords to know which one was which.

"Stop moving!" the Duchess screeched.

"Fine," the Princess paused. "The Jabberwocky can destroy us all!"

"That creature is a legend."

"And yet the Vorpal Blade exists!"

A scuffle at the doors distracted the Duchess and her loyal soldiers. Seizing the moment, Gabby grabbed the crest and ran, disappearing into a hidden passage that led outdoors.

"Get the Princess!" the Duchess shouted.

Holding her breath, Gabby darted down the side tunnel, the one that led towards the Library, before dropping to her knees.

Closing her eyes again, she held her hands over the pommels of the swords before the Vorpal Blade called to her. Sparks of blue quickly filled the air as she pulled the sword from its casing.

"I need a scabbard," the Princess barely dared to whisper before finding one in front of her. Sliding the magical blade into its new scabbard, the tunnel went dark again.

"Did you see that?" the faint voice of one of the Duchess' bodyguards echoed down the tunnel

"No," another voice echoed as the man, a Princess supporter, snapped at the person next to him.

"But something was glowing blue!"

"We saw nothing," the opposing voice hissed.

"Yes, sir."

The sound of booted feet soon passed and Gabby wondered where she should go next.

A tug on her right arm pulled her toward the Library. "Come on, Princess," Ethan's voice whispered in her ear. "My brothers are waiting for us."

"The Jabberwocky is coming."

"We know."

The brothers led her outside, but it was for naught. It didn't take long for the Duchess's loyal soldiers to form a ring around the Princess and seizing her bodyguards.

"Well, look who we have here," the Duchess sighed. "And you boys were locked away tight." Looking at the Princess, she stated. "Must be magic. That magic will be mine when I remove your head from your shoulders."

"I'd like to see you try," Princess Gabrielle growled.

"That can be arranged."

A crying screech pierced the air around the pair. A muffled round of, "It's the Jabberwocky," raced through the crowd surrounding Gabby and the Duchess.

"Maybe," Gabby drawled, "this fight isn't between the two of us."

Scoffing, the Duchess smirked, "You'll need the Vorpal Blade to defeat that creature and nobody knows where that cursed blade is located."

Gabby released a full smile against the Duchess, catching the older woman off guard. "Nobody," she whispered, "except the true heir to the Wonderland Throne." Removing the sword from its scabbard, she revealed the results of her mission. "This was worth getting caught for."

The blade was unimpressive on its own. Nobody suspected that it had been hanging over the throne for Queen Alice of Fifth's entire reign. The grip was simply wrapped in silver wire. No gemstones adorned its hilt. It looked exactly like a practice sword except when Gabby held it aloft for everybody to see gold sparkles filled the air around her. A blue glow overtook the air, bathing Gabby and the Vorpal Blade in its light.

The Crown Princess and true monarch's triumph was short-lived as the shrieking cry of the Jabberwocky once again filled the air.

"Foolish girl," the Duchess cried, reaching for the sword. "All you've done is inform me where to find the blade. Thank you." Snatching the sword away from Gabby, the Duchess was left confused when the blue glow faded. "No. No. No," she repeated. "This cannot be happening. Glow! I'm the rightful Queen!" She shook the sword as if that would bring back the golden sparkles and blue aura.

A sudden gust of wind messed up the Duchess's perfectly coifed hair. She wasn't expecting a fight. She wasn't expecting the legend to be real. It was supposed to be simply a legend.

"Who dares disturb my rest?" the booming, smoky voice hissed.

Turning carefully to face her new opponent, the Duchess shrieked at the monster in front of her. Dragon-like, its face looked like a fish with whiskers, scales covered its body, and giant claws gripped the earth between its talons. The Jabberwocky's tail was long enough to demolish several painted rose bushes twenty-five feet away.

Unknowing, she missed how everybody was pointing at her.

"False Queen of Wonderland," the Jabberwocky stated, focusing on the impractically dressed Duchess. "You are charged with the murder of the King of Wonderland, the unlawful execution of the former Queen of Wonderland, the obstruction of the crowning of the new Queen of Wonderland, and the imprisonment and oppression of the residents of Wonderland. How do you plead?"

"I wasn't aware this was a trial. What gives you the right?" the Duchess screeched.

Sighing, the Princess rolled her eyes before answering, "Even I know this. The Jabberwocky is the source of the Queen's powers. He is the scales of justice and right. The Jabberwocky is all-knowing and omniscient. As soon as you murdered my parents you awakened the beast." Bowing to the Jabberwocky, Gabby showed her respect towards the terrifying monster.

"And yet she holds the Blade," the beast growled.

"Theft," Ethan spoke up. "She stole the sword from the Princess. You can see it isn't even glowing for her."

Glancing at the Duchess, the Jabberwocky concurred, "In the right hands there should be sparkles and an aura."

Sighing, several townspeople and Cards darted out of the path of the Jabberwocky's fiery breath.

"I am older and wiser than my angry ancient grandmother. My egg has been laid and is due to hatch any moment now. The true Queen of Wonderland will be able to defeat me in battle. Oh, False Queen, since you hold the Vorpal Sword, you shall go first. Defeat me or face a fiery end."

Trembling, the Duchess stood before the monster.

"Have your blade ready," a soldier shouted at her.

"Hush," another one told the other.

"No!" Gabby shouted, rushing towards the beast. "She murdered my parents. Her punishment is my responsibility."

"Very well."

"Gabby!" Ethan shouted. "Watch out!"

Drawing an average blade from a scabbard at her side, Gabby quickly parried the Duchess' wild thrust.

"This is my throne," panted the Duchess.

"This is my birthright," Gabby retorted back, careful to keep her guard and balance against the wildly attacking Duchess. "These are my people. This is my legacy. Not. Yours."

Seeing an opening, Gabby thrust her sword, finding the soft belly of the Duchess's body. Moments later, the Jabberwocky snapped the Duchess' neck with her teeth. "I simply cannot take simpering and whining as the mortally wounded beg and plead for their lives," she explained. "I'd rather hear screaming in pain that stops abruptly."

Moving forward, Ethan approached with the Vorpal Blade stretched out in his hands from where he'd retrieved it from the ground. "Your Majesty, Your Jabberwockiness, the Vorpal Sword."

Gabby reached for the sword. "Are you certain?" she asked even as the blue aura returned.

"With each generation comes a new Jabberwocky," the beast explained. "When your grandmother passed away in her sleep my mother slowly faded away. Then I was hatched on the ascension of your mother. Do you understand?"

Gulping, Gabby whispered, "You must die as my mother died."

"Yes, My Queen," the Jabberwocky bowed her head.

Expecting a spray of blood, Gabby swung to cut off the Jabberwocky's neck. Instead, she heard, *May you live long and die peacefully,* as the beast disappeared into smoke.

Everybody around her cheered except for Ethan. He understood her silence. Dropping the blade, Gabby sunk to her knees and started sobbing. Pulling her into his arms, Ethan rocked back and forth while the townspeople watched the pair. A faint blue glow encircled Gabby while a darker blue started to form around Ethan. One by one the townspeople dropped to their knees and bowed their heads.

"Your Majesties," a purring voice caught their attention. "I have the pleasure to introduce the future Queen of Wonderland, the Crown Princess Gabrielle and her Royal Consort Ethan Jackson."

Burrowing her head into his chest, Gabby whispered, "I told you so."

Chuckling, "Yes you did," Ethan agreed.

Chapter 26

He wasn't exactly certain how he found himself standing next to Gabby. Wonderland had spoken, and a Spade had become the Queen's Consort.

"Do you Gabrielle Harrington Erickson swear to put Wonderland's best interests in your heart and decisions and treat its citizens with the respect they deserve?"

It was easy to tune out. Ethan had never found himself standing in front of so many people before, and he was trying not to fidget as the Princess faced her coronation.

"Do you swear to be a benevolent Queen, a merciful and just monarch?"

"I swear."

He felt their eyes on him, wondering why a Card and Huntsman had been declared Consort and why their own sons weren't worthy of the Queen's heart.

It wasn't something he could explain. Maybe it was the Tracker's Bond. Maybe it was the weeks he spent beside her in the classroom or their time together during Gabby's trials in the Enchanted Forest. Ethan could only acknowledge the bond that had formed between them was bigger than he had once thought.

Kings and Princes from other kingdoms were eyeing him, wondering why a commoner was able to assume the throne instead of one of their second sons. It was easy to forget that the Forest and lands easily found ways to reward the deserving.

"I, your Majesties' Heart and head advisor now crown thee the Queen of Wonderland if you accept the honor."

"I accept."

There was complete silence when the Heart bade the Princess to kneel before him. Dress billowing around her, Gabby lowered herself to her knees, head rose proudly. The intake of breath was audible as the Heart lowered the Queen's Crown unto her head. Gabby was now Gabrielle, the Tenth Queen of Wonderland.

Everything shifted as she rose. As soon as the scepter was handed over the shifting settled and everything was calm.

"Do you, Ethan Samuel Jackson Huntsman Spade accept the role of Queen's Consort?"

"I do."

"Do you swear to protect the crown, the Queen, and the Queen's heir with your life?"

"I swear."

"Do you promise to defend Wonderland, its people, and its traditions as long as you are the Royal Consort?"

"I promise."

"Kneel."

Kneeling in front of his brother was an interesting experience. The last time he had kneeled in front of anybody was when he was sworn in as a Huntsman.

"I, the Queen's Heart, now declare you to be the Queen's Consort." A lightweight band was placed on Ethan's head at his brother's words.

Before the coronation, Gabby – Gabrielle – had explained that they didn't have to be married to crown him as her Consort. "It just means the intention is there." But he knew that if they waited too long then Wonderland would become unsettled again. It might start off small – a failed harvest or missing cattle - before becoming massive – flooding and disease.

"We won't wait. Coronation first, wedding second."

"Are you certain?" she had asked him.

"Positive, but I have to do something first." Grabbing her, he kissed Gabby for the second time. Her arms had circled his neck, a hand snaking into his hair. His hands had settled on her waist before they started to explore her curves. "I've wanted to do that ever since I found you in the Ballroom." He had whispered once they finally broke apart. "And I didn't want our second kiss to be on our wedding day."

"Agreed," she had whispered, pulling him back towards her.

But they'd agreed that Gabby's coronation was more important than their wedding. The settling everybody felt as soon as she assumed the mantle was unmistakable. They knew that it wouldn't be easy. The after-effects of the Duchess's coup were still being found throughout Wonderland. Patches of the land refused to grow. Some minor flooding had threatened a few homes. It was a warning from the land and it scared Gabby more than anything.

"What if I'm not a good Queen," she'd whispered in the dark.

"Then Wonderland will tell you," Ethan whispered back.

And now she was wearing the crown and Wonderland had approved of her ascension.

But there had been no shifting and settling when the silver band had been placed on Ethan's head and that left him worried.

Leaning forward, the Heart whispered, "You aren't married yet. Wonderland knows you have a history of leaving her and it won't be completely settled until you are married."

This meant uncertainty and discord. This meant that certain members of the town would wait, or help, the new couple fall apart before flying in like vultures to harvest the carcass of their failed relationship.

And from the look in the Queen's eyes, Ethan realized that she knew it too.

"Tomorrow," he stated.

"Tomorrow," she agreed.

"Tomorrow it is," the Heart concluded. "I'll speak with Father Liddell."

Chapter 27

Mary was behind her, playing with Gabby's hair while they waited on a maid. Her rounded belly was just starting to become noticeable. "Do we have to have the talk about what you should expect tonight?" A flush raced across Mary's face at her words.

Gabby reassured her sister-in-law, "The Harrington's made sure I was aware of what would happen when I was starting to show interest in boys. They had advised me to wait because it was more than just losing my virginity." Staring in the mirror, she sighed, "My whole life they gave me little clues like that in an attempt to prepare me for Wonderland."

Shaking her head, she continued, "My friends never understood why I waited, but it never felt right with any of my ex-boyfriends."

That was when the maid entered carrying a light blue dress. "A dress fit for a Queen," she stated. "It took the tailors hours to make it perfect." Shaking it out, she held the dress up for the royals to see.

"Oh my," was Gabby's reaction, her thoughts escaping her completely.

"It's perfect," Mary sighed.

It was. The light blue dress had dark blue spades scattered around the skirt and bodice. "For His Consort's Suit," the maid explained.

Small diamonds twinkled in the folds of the skirt among the tiny rubies and onyx. The hem and top of the bodice were lined with red and black suits. Every aspect of Wonderland and its founding families were represented on the dress.

"It's amazing."

"They've been working on it ever since you returned home, but they pulled an all-nighter on the blue spades and making certain that the dress would fit your measurements," the maid informed them as she hung it up and started opening the tiny hooks that closed the dress.

Giggling, Mary whispered, "Ethan will hate those hooks."

"Good," Gabby responded. "Not everything needs to be easy."

Spotting the Harrington's outside the archway that led into the church, Gabby burst into tears. "I never thought I'd ever see you again!"

"Your Ethan sent some trackers to find us. They explained what was going on and stated you needed somebody to walk you down the aisle," Michaela Harrington explained.

"I'd be honored," Preston answered, revealing how choked up he was becoming. "I only wish your biological parents were here too. I've always wanted to meet them."

"I wish they were here too."

The church was covered in white roses – not a single red rose was in sight – and blue forget-me-nots. Mary and Michaela had spent hours helping the maids decorate the church the night before. Gabby couldn't figure out how they knew…

"I remember your wedding binder from when you were dating what's-his-name," Michaela explained. "I knew it couldn't have changed that much."

Henry slipped into the room, "Can we get a move on, Your Majesty?" The Heart asked. "You have a nervous groom waiting." After the ceremony, Stephan would once again become her head bodyguard, even though Henry was the Head Card.

"Henry, you are about to become my brother-in-law – you can call me Gabby," she insisted. "Just give me a moment then we can open the doors for the impatient and hopeful audience."

"And so, Ethan can breathe again," Henry chuckled, more than happy to be off official Card duty for a little while.

Looking at the room around her, Gabby gazed at the white tulle gathered at the end of each pew with a dark blue bow. There was no unity candle or sand that would be poured into a vessel; the ceremony the day before had already joined them together. There was no canopy or bower or anything else over their heads that would make her sneeze.

No, everybody would see only them and Father Liddell and that was exactly what she wanted.

Slipping through a side door, they could see a guard opening the doors to the waiting crowd of Wonderlandians, Royals, Cards, and Huntsmen. There was a swell of noise before it was shut off by the shutting of a door.

"How much longer?" The Queen sighed, wondering if she could use her powers to push forward the ceremony.

"Only a quarter of an hour," Mary whispered.

"I can wait fifteen minutes," she stated, even if each minute felt like forever. "I've already waited this long."

Also Available by this Author:

Standalones
The Secrets Between Us

The Magic Chronicles
Half-Moon Manor (Olivia and Henry's Story)
Keeping Secrets

The Hastings Sisters Novels
The Consequences of Being Aiden (Ainsley's story)
The Trouble with Chasing Aileen
The Problem with Finding Ashlynn
Untitled Aiden's Story (Coming Soon)

The Enchanted Forest
Into the Enchanted Forest
The Cursed Garden
The Bewitched Tower (Coming Soon)
Ander and the Cocky Dragon Slayer

The Bookworm Next Door Series
Stephanie Makes the Match
The Party
The Bookworm's Makeover
The Bookworm Next Door
Along the Road
Near the Finish Line

The Summer After Graduation
The Bookworm Next Door: The High School Stories Collection

The Jane Austen Variations
Persuaded (Persuasion)
First Impressions (Coming Soon)

About the Author

Alicia Chumney has her B.A. in English Literature and her 7-12 English teacher certification. Since middle school she has been scribbling in notebooks, on scrap paper, even in a restaurant ticket book one time (she still has the ticket book).

She lives in Tennessee with her cat, Molly, and a stack of books that she doubts she will finish reading in her lifetime. This is mostly because she spends a fair amount of time rereading her favorite books: Anne of Green Gables and Pride and Prejudice.

You can find her on:
Facebook
Twitter
Goodreads

Made in the USA
Middletown, DE
14 September 2021